THE
THIRD
DAY

ANNE BARTON

The Third Day
Anne Barton

Carrick Publishing
Print Edition 2014
ISBN 13: 978-1-927114-995
Cover Design by Sara Carrick

This book is dedicated to Randy and Nancy.

He ... was crucified, died and was buried.
He descended to the dead.
On the third day he rose again.
He ascended into heaven,
and is seated at the right hand of the Father.

From The Apostles' Creed

PROLOGUE

"Ah, yes. I'm feeling on top of the world tonight." He spoke the words with obvious relish as he poured drinks for himself and his visitor. "I've got it all figured out."

"Got what all figured out?" his guest asked.

"I've uncovered a fine little fiddle, I have. Not so little, either. A few thousands here, a few thousands there, a few thousands somewhere else. Neat scheme, too. Would have got away with it if it weren't for my computerized accounting business. Faxes and all that. Modems. Companies too small to have their own accounting departments, but too big for the boss's wife to do it. Can transmit all their stuff directly to me and I can do their accounts faster than they could. Payroll too. Nice business."

"What sort of a fiddle?" The guest's voice betrayed a guarded anxiety that the host failed altogether to notice. Too bad for him.

"Someone's created a false company. Sends invoices to other companies, gets payment. All make believe. Does it to small companies back east, one's that have a bad record of inefficiency. That is, before they started using my services. Don't know how many. Found one last month. Thought it odd. Found another last week. Suspicious. Then Saturday, a third. Aha!"

"What made you notice them?" The voice was taut, cold, ominous.

"Fake company is local—here in Exeter. No company. No name. Cancelled cheques just stamped on the back. But the bank will know. Bank of Vancouver. Got all the data together. Tomorrow I go to the bank. They won't tell me, but they'll tell the police."

The guest was silent.

The host turned, drinks in hand, reaching out to offer one to his visitor. For one awful moment before the bullet slammed into his chest, ending his life, he knew the identity of the person he had been tracking.

ONE

"God, I wish he'd shut up!" I muttered to Penny Farnham, who was sitting beside me on the blue-grey, velour-covered couch whose cushions enveloped us in their soft embrace. She nodded in silent agreement as she tossed a great mop of brown hair back from her comely, pink-cheeked face.

We were attending the twice-monthly bible study group that met at the home of Harry and Shirley Meacham in the fashionable Victoria Hill section of Exeter, a small city in the interior of British Columbia. Owen Dunphy, a regular attendee of the bible sessions, had gotten off on his pet subject: homosexuals in the Bible.

"No one should have told him about John Spong's book," Penny whispered in reply.

I snorted. "Even if Spong does suggest that St. Paul might have been gay, he certainly didn't carry the subject to the extremes that Owen does."

Owen was well underway, his voice rising as he talked, the tone of fanatical conviction evident in the forcefulness of his speech, the way he leaned forward in his chair, a clenched fist pounding his knee. "It's well known that the Greeks were a homosexual bunch. And there were lots of Greeks in the Holy Land. Greek was one of the major languages. Everyone used it."

"Many educated people used Greek," Paul St. Cyr, a retired journalist, interposed. "The peasant classes spoke Aramaic."

"Or Hebrew," Shirley Meacham suggested.

"Not even Hebrew. That was the language of the educated Jews." Paul, a small, slender man with thinning white hair, casually crossed his legs and leaned back comfortably in the armchair which was a companion to the couch enfolding Penny and me.

Owen showed no evidence of having heard. He barely paused before continuing his oration. "The Bible wouldn't be full of exhortations not to engage in homosexual practices if they weren't common. Those Greeks…"

"Most of the exhortations you're talking about were in the early parts of the Old Testament and there weren't any Greeks around at that time." Paul pulled himself out of the soft cushion and leaned forward, prepared to do battle.

"You're wrong, Paul, you're wrong. Jesus was always talking about homosexuality."

"Where?"

"Matthew 15 for one."

"That is about adultery and fornication." The speaker this time was Linda Meacham, the daughter of Shirley and Harry. I had first met her this evening, as she was home from university for the Easter break. I remembered having heard that she was studying theology, and hoped to become a priest, but Owen either didn't know or didn't care. He plunged on.

"And Mark 7."

"That's also about adultery and fornication," Linda challenged.

Owen waved his square, rough-skinned hand in dismissal. "Same difference. What I'm saying is …"

"It is *not* the same!"

For once, Owen was brought up short. Grey eyes beneath ridgey brows, topped by an unruly shock of grey hair, widened in surprise. He stared at Linda, who leaned forward in her straight-backed chair, elbows on knees, hands clasped under her chin. She was slim and pretty in a plain, natural way, with even features, a creamy complexion and softly waved brown hair, cut short. She wore jeans and a T-shirt. Her stockinged feet were planted firmly on the floor, and there was an uncompromising quality about her that should have indicated to Owen that he had no chance of winning the argument.

Bravo, I thought, wishing that Linda didn't have to go back to her studies at Vancouver School of Theology before the next bible study session. Nothing I had ever said had any impact on

4

Owen, whose opinions were as firm as his heavy-set frame. He would merely say, in that condescending voice reserved by overbearing men for women who have the temerity to interject an opinion, "Now, Robin, you just don't understand."

He was probably right most of the time, I had to admit. I had only recently come to believe in God and to accept the Christian faith. Having lacked a Christian upbringing, I was woefully ignorant about the Bible and rarely dared even to express a theological opinion. Nevertheless, I resented Owen's attitude. Now, here was a woman, twenty years my junior, taking him on and for once stilling his torrent of words.

Owen changed his tack. Unfortunately, this got him onto another subject I would just as soon he left alone: his military service. "I know all about the Greeks. When I was in Cyprus (with the peacekeeping forces, you know) I was constantly having to tell the young officers they sent over, who were as green as grass, what the Greeks were all about."

"I bet they loved that!" I interjected.

"Well, as a matter of fact they didn't," Owen said, taking my words at face value. "They could get real snotty about a corporal telling them how to behave."

"It's a wonder you weren't thrown in the brig, or whatever they call it in the army."

"They wouldn't have dared because I knew what I was saying. I've always been like that. Always stick to your convictions. To get back to homosexuals, we had a young priest up in Kluane Junction, in the Yukon, when I was there, who carried this love-your-neighbour stuff to the extreme and said we ought to welcome gays in the church. I had to set him straight on that. He always thanked me for it afterward."

"I'll bet," I muttered, but Owen didn't hear me.

"These young guys all have liberal attitudes until they get out in the real world. They have to learn. I've always thought the sooner they did the better, so I always did my Christian duty and took it upon myself to correct them."

5

He should have looked at Linda Meacham. A dark scowl clouded her pretty features and her body had gone rigid. I could see that she wasn't going to let any Owen Dunphy clones tell her what to think when she became a priest. Right then she looked ready and able to fell him with a swift karate chop.

Harry Meacham cleared his throat and rustled the sheath of papers he held in his lap. He was a man of medium height and build, in his early sixties, his crinkly grey hair neatly styled. He looked soft and pink, "I think we should get back to our bible study," Harry suggested, his voice gentle but firm.

"Yes we should," Owen agreed. "As I was saying, Jesus preached against homosexuality. I've heard people argue that Jesus himself had a homosexual relationship with the disciple John, but I don't believe it for a minute. Now John, in his Gospel, might have said on several occasions that he was the disciple Jesus loved, but I think that was just egotism."

"You're confusing love and sex. They aren't synonymous," I said. "I read somewhere that the Greek word 'caritas ' can be translated either as 'love' or as 'charity' and is really somewhere in between, something that English doesn't have a word for. 'Compassion' may come as close as anything."

"I don't care what it says in Greek. And I don't hold with these new translations. The King James Version, and it's the only one that matters as far as I'm concerned, says…"

"The King James Version is a translation from a translation from a translation."

Linda smiled at my terse tone, recognizing a fellow-sufferer. "Actually, only a translation of a translation when it comes to the New Testament. It was written entirely in Greek. The Old Testament, which is also known as the Hebrew Scriptures, was as you might suppose, written in Hebrew."

"After being handed down orally for generations covering hundreds of years before any of it was written down," I added. This was one thing I did know about the Bible.

"The earlier books, yes."

6

"Anyway, the KJV is a translation into medieval English from the Latin Vulgate, which was translated from Greek. So you can't nit-pick about individual words." When it came to historical fact, not theology, I felt that I was on solid ground.

"Right!" Linda gave a sharp nod to her head as if to punctuate her remark. "Furthermore, it wasn't the only translation into English in the middle ages, but it was the one that caught on."

We both stared defiantly at Owen.

Don Urquhart, who had been silent until now, uncoiled his long frame from his chair. "Look. I've got to leave. I have to be up early in the morning."

"Let's have a break," Shirley, our matronly hostess, suggested. "There's tea and coffee and some brownies in the kitchen. You can all help yourselves."

"If there are some of Shirley's brownies," Don licked his lips, "I'll stay a little longer."

We all shuffled into the kitchen in our stocking feet and helped ourselves to beverages and brownies. I've always felt funny about taking my shoes off at the door. I'd never lived with people who did that, but after attending meetings for the last year or so in parishioners' spotless houses, which looked as if they were never lived in except when some group from St. Matthew's Anglican Church met there, I could see why. In my own house, another muddy footprint for the housekeeper to clean up was merely a part of the decor. There were faint spots on the light-green carpet where my big fat white cat, Cloud Nine, had thrown up an occasional hairball and the liquid part had soaked in before I had found it, often by stepping on it at night with my bare feet. I could never get the carpet really clean. The well-traveled areas were beginning to be a bit threadbare. My house wasn't really dirty. It just looked lived in.

I felt at home in Penny Farnham's place. It was spotlessly clean, as befits a public health nurse, but there were usually newspapers strewn on the floor, outer garments dropped casually on the backs of furniture, and piles of papers on the dining room table. In other words, it resembled mine. As I glanced about Mrs. Meacham's surgically clean kitchen, it occurred to me that we never met in the homes of people with children. They probably didn't want to go to the effort of getting their houses in the kind of shape the older parishioners seemed to cherish.

If the houses were spotlessly neat, the people weren't. We were attired in an assortment of sweat suits and jeans, of T-shirts, sweat tops and flannel shirts. Most of the shoes piled up near the door were battered joggers. There was one exception to this air of scruffiness. One small, white-haired lady was clad in an exquisitely tailored suit of light grey with straight skirt and form-fitting jacket, over a richly flowered blouse. Faith LaBounty never expressed disapproval of the style of dress of anyone else, but I had always thought that perhaps she had turned up at the wrong meeting. She would remove a pair of slippers from her purse and put them on after removing her shoes at the door. This seemed unnecessary, as I'm sure no speck of dirt would have the audacity to cling to Faith LaBounty's immaculate and expensive shoes.

Shirley Meacham trotted over to where I was standing, coffee cup in one hand and a rich, gooey brownie in the other. She had Linda in tow. "Linda, I'd like you to meet Robin Carruthers, the pilot I was telling you about."

"Oh!" Linda's hazel eyes lit up. "I've been dying to meet you. Mum and Dad have told me so much about you. You teach flying, don't you?"

"Yes. I run Red Robin Flying School."

"Red Robin. How did you hit on that name?"

"It was a nickname I had when I was a teen-ager, because of my red hair." I'm a regular carrot-top, my short wind-blown locks crowning a face that reddens easily. I'm tall for a woman, in my mid-forties, beginning to put on a bit of unwanted weight about the middle. I dress in browns and greens, the only colours that don't clash with my hair and my complexion, and my clothes are of the practical type, ones from which I can wash the oil stains from the airplanes I work with.

"I see. It's pretty appropriate. I'd like to learn how to fly one of these days, but if I become a priest, I don't suppose I'll be able to afford it."

"I've heard of several priests who fly. Some of them up in the North have to."

"Brrr!" Linda shivered. "I hope I never get sent up there. Especially not to Kluane Junction." We both turned to look toward the opposite side of the room where Owen had poor little Faith LaBounty cornered, and shared a knowing laugh. "Anyway, I'll be attached to this diocese, since I've been sponsored by Bishop Michael, and he will have the say over where I go."

"Really? I thought each church decided on who they want. I remember that we interviewed Douglas and decided we wanted him." I could distinctly remember the night of that interview with the Reverend Douglas Forsythe, our rector. He had made a very favourable impression on us, especially me, even though I had no inkling at the time of the impact he would have on my life.

"Yes, but Bishop Michael sent him. At least there are no really horrendous places in this diocese. I'd be glad to go to any of them."

"Maybe he'll assign you here as our curate."

"No. One is never sent to one's hometown. Too stressful."

"Well, at least that means you won't have to put up with Owen Dunphy."

She sighed. "I've been working on this Christian charity, or love, bit. Sometimes it's difficult."

My thoughts wandered back to Owen and Faith. Poor Faith! I was sure she hadn't a clue as to what Owen was raving about. I thought she only came to the bible study in order to have some social life. I wasn't sure whether she was a widow or a spinster, this tiny, pale, white-haired, sad-eyed wraith of a woman. Her clothing was simple, neat and very expensive. I remembered another parishioner who worked at a pricey dress shop on Main Street telling me that Faith had come to the shop to buy a new spring outfit, complete with hat and gloves, and had never once looked at a price tag. Nor had she checked the total on her Visa Gold Card before signing it. She had moved to Exeter about two years ago, from Winnipeg, had quietly appeared in church but never took part in the activities that the central core of the parish were constantly engaged in. It was months before she could be persuaded even to come to the coffee hour after church. She seemed very uneasy around men and shunned their company unless there were several women around to cushion the impact.

She didn't participate in the bible study discussions, only listened. After tonight, I thought, she'll never come again.

The doorbell rang and Harry went to answer it. I heard a booming male voice with an accent that might have been Australian ask, "Is Faith LaBounty here? Have I got the right place?"

"Yes, she's here. Come on in."

Faith rose hastily to her feet and almost ran to the door, leaving Owen open-mouthed in mid-sentence.

"Clive! Do come in." She grasped the man's large, red hand between her two small dainty white ones and drew him into the room. "Let me introduce you to my friends. They are all from the church."

She turned toward the roomful of people, her face glowing, animation which I had never seen before emanating from every fibre of her body. "This is my friend, Clive Hawthorne."

There was a cheerful chorus of mixed voices as we welcomed the stranger. "Are you an old Exonian, or are you new here?" Paul asked.

"I'm from Edmonton. I just moved here to get away from Alberta winters." Clive Hawthorne grimaced and we all laughed. Many of us had come to Exeter for exactly that reason. Clive went on, "Actually, I'm from all over northern Alberta. I was in the oil business. I just retired. Thought I'd get away from those prairie winters," he said cheerfully, then dropped his voice to a lower register and added sorrowfully, "and to get away from constant reminders of my late wife."

We expressed suitable sympathy. Faith drew him into the kitchen and plied him with coffee and brownies, which he enthused about, heaping praise upon Shirley, the hostess. He was a large man; tall, moderately overweight, of indeterminate age but probably around Owen's age, about sixty, with sandy hair that had recently seen a first-class hairdresser, and pale blue eyes. He was clad in neat and expensive brown slacks, an open-necked sport shirt and a light brown cashmere sweater. He reeked of money. Faith clung to him; he looked down at her with a benign smile and put his arm decorously about her frail shoulders.

"I'm happy to meet folks who are friends of this lovely little lady. My life has sure changed since I've met her. I've been sad and lonely since I lost my dear wife, and Faith has put the joy back in my life. She's so loving and kind, and so good to me."

Faith beamed up at him, her usually pale face highlighted with radiant colour.

"Wow! What's got into Faith?"

I turned and looked down to see Penny at my side, her brown eyes wide with wonder, and replied, "I was asking myself the same question."

"He's certainly made little old Faith sparkle."

That he had. In minutes, his presence had accomplished a miraculous transformation that we as an entire parish had been unable to achieve in the two years she had been among us. Faith had positively blossomed with animation before our admiring eyes.

Why then, I wondered, had I taken such an instant dislike to him?

TWO

The following day, Tuesday of Holy Week, was not a good day for flying. Two students who had not reached the stage in their training where doing circuits would be beneficial to them, lounged around waiting for the weather to get better. Terry McGregor, one of my experienced instructors, had taken another student out in one of our red and white Cessna 150 trainers to do takeoffs and landings, the only training exercise that was feasible on this day of low ceilings and intermittent rain. Watching them through the window of my office, which looked out over the rain-washed field, I was reminded of the British phrase for this stage of flight training, "circuits and bumps." The bumps were quite obvious, as this student hadn't yet got the hang of flaring out smoothly so that the wings lost their lift just when the wheels touched the ground. Landing is an art. It requires a "feel" that this fellow, who was in the early stages of his training, hadn't yet mastered.

First, he would fly into the ground, creating a big bounce that had to be retrieved by adding power. Overcompensating, he would then flare out too high and drop the plane onto the runway. I could sense his frustration and the patient, gentle teaching of Terry, the instructor.

None of my instructors are allowed to use the insult-and-threat method of instructing. Patience and praise work better. Positive motivations work better than negative ones. Setting a good example is another powerful teaching tool, and I now saw this in practice. I could tell from the plane's much less erratic course, that Terry had temporarily taken over, having the student "follow through" on the controls. Set up for a stable approach, the small trainer descended evenly toward the runway. Over the threshold, the one-fifty was only a few metres above the surface. I watched the nose come up slowly and smoothly. As the plane slowed, the increased lift created by the change in the angle at which the wing met the air kept it flying level, just above the ground. The slower speed caused the wing to lose more of its lift, so the angle had to be constantly increased, until finally the wing stalled, losing its lift, and the 150 settled the last few inches onto the runway. The airflow over the horizontal tail surfaces still gave control around the lateral axis, and I could see that Terry was holding full up-elevator, delaying the moment when the nose wheel finally settled onto the runway, all the while creating maximum aerodynamic braking. When the nose wheel finally touched down, the 150 was almost at a stop in the mild headwind.

They taxied off the runway and moved back toward the departure end. I could see Terry in the right seat, talking to the student, using hand gestures to make his point. I could visualize myself in that cockpit. I'd been there thousands of times before, coaching hundreds of students through these manoeuvres, in over twenty years of teaching people to fly. It is one of the most rewarding occupations in the world.

Through my office's open doorway, I saw the two lounging students look at the clock, realize that enough time had passed that a new weather report would be available, go to the phone and dial the Flight Service Station over in Pine Hill. They took turns talking on the phone, and I could tell by their glum expressions and the sag of their shoulders that the news was not favourable. I had already told them that the forecast was not good enough for beginning students to fly that day, but I never object to pilots calling up to find out for themselves. We tried to instil into them the habit of checking the weather, and insisted they do so before every flight. The two students reluctantly gave up and went home.

I swivelled my chair back toward the window, propped my long legs, crossed at the ankles, on the desktop, clasped my hands behind my head, and engaged in the favourite pastime of ground-bound aviators: watching other pilots land. I could justify this seemingly aimless pursuit by telling myself I needed to observe how the students and instructors at my school were doing.

Terry's student was making some progress. After one fairly decent landing, they taxied in. They tied down the trainer, the only one that had been out. Now all six of the identically painted red and white planes were sitting forlornly on their tiedown spots in the drizzling rain.

I generally used such dismal days to catch up on paperwork, but that morning, my mind would not stay on the task. I had a vague feeling of things not being right, of something left undone. Not here at Red Robin Flying School. Everything seemed to be under control. Nothing was happening. It was just a depressing, dreary day. Even the ducks that sat on the street in front of my house when I had left for work that morning had waddled in a slow, dejected procession to the side of the street to let me back my Ford Ranger pickup out of my driveway. As I had waited for them, I had imagined Cloud Nine licking his lips and wishing he were allowed outside.

Something else then. Something hanging onto the very edge of my memory, which, when I went in search of it, slipped quietly away. I thought back to the previous night. I certainly hadn't got much out of the bible study session, except a headache! I'd started to attend only a short time before, thinking I ought to delve into the Bible, which was unfamiliar territory to me, more deeply than I could do on my own. But I wasn't going to learn anything worthwhile the way it went last night. My faith was still as shaky as a tree house built by eight-year-olds, and to have to listen for two hours to Owen Dunphy's opinionated pronouncements, might knock down the fragile edifice of my fledgling faith. People like Owen, with the attitudes they expressed, had made me avoid church throughout most of my adult life.

Perhaps, I mused, I should have a talk with our rector, the Reverend Douglas Forsythe, the man who had been instrumental in starting me on the path of conversion. He'd be busy this week, though. It would have to wait until after Easter.

The phone rang and Joyce, the morning dispatcher, the only other person on duty that morning, answered it. "It's for you, Robin," she called, and I picked up the receiver on my desk.

"Hi." Penny's sprightly voice greeted me. "What did you think of last night?"

I groaned and Penny laughed. "I agree. I wish we could find some way to get Owen out of the group so we can follow the study guide. Got any ideas?"

"What evening does he have something else to do so he can't come? We could change our night."

"I don't think that would work. He'd feel that it was his duty in life to be sure he was there to set us straight."

"We could murder him."

"I think that's a bit drastic."

"Well, either he goes, or I do," I stated vehemently.

"I don't blame you. I think I'll stick it out for a while yet, though."

"I'll come one more time," I declared. "But after that, I'm out if I'm going to have to put up with that."

"Owen's leading Compline Sunday night. Did you know? Douglas is taking a few day's break after Easter, starting right after the morning services are over."

"He needs a break, but how come Owen is leading Compline? Why don't we just skip it for one week? Not many people come, anyway."

I heard Penny's lively laugh come over the phone. "I think that was what Douglas had planned, but when he said so, Owen told him that he used to lead services in Kluane Junction the weeks when they didn't have a priest. So, since Douglas is always after us to get involved in things, he couldn't very well turn down Owen's offer."

"You can count me out this Sunday, then. I'm not going to go if Owen is going to lead it."

"Me either. How about going out to the buffet at the Lakeview Terrace?"

"Sounds great. You've got a date."

Penny's voice changed its tone. "Speaking of dates," she said conspiratorially, "what did you think of Faith's?"

Should I say what I thought? I decided I should. Penny was my best friend and I could trust her discretion. "Not much," I said guardedly.

"You don't like him?" There was a note of incredulity in Penny's exclamation.

"I don't know why, but there's something about him that makes me uneasy."

"I think that if either one of them gets let down, it will be Clive. He seems so lively, and she's such a mouse."

"I guess that's why I think something's wrong. I can't imagine a guy like that falling for a woman like Faith."

"He wants to protect her."

I sighed. "I hope you're right, but I have the feeling he's what she needs to be protected from." My feet, clad in soft brown Hush Puppies, were perched comfortably atop my desk, as I looked out toward the rain-drenched runway at a silver Dash 8 commuter plane that had struggled down through the overcast. It had broken out of the clouds right at minimums. A rooster tail of spray followed it down the runway, gradually subsiding as the plane rolled to a stop.

"Oh, don't be such a grouch!" Penny exclaimed and I laughed. "I've never seen her look so happy. Don't knock it." I could visualize Penny brushing the great mass of brown hair back from her attractive young face, a characteristic gesture that served to instantly identify her.

"Okay, I won't," I promised.

As I hung up, I heard the chatter of happy voices in the outer office. Joyce called to me, "Ralph and Eve are here. They want to talk to you."

Ralph Thompson, a retired contractor who had made a small fortune during Exeter's building boom, flew his own light twin-engine airplane, a Twin Comanche. Eve, his wife and constant flying companion, had gone through our "Pinch Hitter" course, designed to teach non-pilots how to take over in an emergency. She also did the navigating, and was quite good at it.

Ralph, a jovial fellow with a heavyset body that was running to fat now that he wasn't heaving bundles of shingles onto roofs or lifting twelve-foot walls into place, was in conversation with Terry, telling him about the fishing resort he had discovered. "You ought to set up a regular run out there, charter people in," he was telling Terry, who looked decidedly interested. "Great fishing. They'll supply all the tackle if you don't have your own. Boats, guides, place to smoke your catch, everything. There's a big lodge and small individual cabins. If you want everything done for you, you stay in the lodge. If you want to rough it a bit, you get a cabin. A buddy of mine and I discovered it last summer."

I remembered his enthusiasm over his find. At an open house we had held shortly after his trip, he had shown a video he had taken. It was the usual corny home video, except for the flying part, which his buddy had shot during their landing approach to the immaculate grass strip on the shore of a pristine sub-Arctic lake.

"My buddy and I went in there ourselves the first time, but we were so nose heavy coming out with all that fish stowed in the nose compartment, we decided we'd have to take the girls next time, to put some weight farther back in the plane."

"Ralph!" Ralph turned to look at Eve, his mouth hanging open. She stood there, hands on ample hips, brow furrowed, glowering as if deciding whether to have him drawn and quartered or merely hung by the heels for several hours.

"What's the matter, dear?" he asked in a small, obsequious voice.

"You do not tell ladies that you take them along for ballast!"

That cracked us all up, and the day brightened considerably.

After Eve had suitably put Ralph in his place, she turned to me. "Robin, we had this wonderful idea. We hope you can get away this weekend. Ralph wants to do some more instrument flying and get updated. We thought it would be nice to fly down to Vegas for the weekend. You could give him instruction, and we'd all get a chance to lie around in the sun. It's been pretty gloomy around here lately."

"I couldn't go this weekend."

"Joyce said you didn't have anything on that couldn't be re-scheduled for another time. If you're worried about money, we'd pay all your expenses. We'd even give you some to gamble with if you want."

"I don't gamble," I said, and could have added that a trip to the crowded, garish tourist trap that was Las Vegas was about as appealing as horseradish ice cream.

"You don't have to gamble. There are lots of other things to do. You can just lie around in the sun."

Lying around doing nothing sounded even less attractive than gambling, though it had the advantage of being cheap. I'm a vigorous, restless person. I want to be on the go, doing something active and interesting. I'm not a museum-goer, a poolside people-watcher or a couch potato. Meditation, breakfast in bed and tedious tea parties are as welcome as a dip in Lake Devon, which lay adjacent to the city of Exeter, in January.

"I can't go this weekend, anyway."

"Why not? Joyce says things are slow." Eve turned toward Joyce's desk. "Isn't that right?"

Joyce nodded. "Why don't you go?"

"It's not that," I told them. "It's Easter."

"All the more reason to go with us. You'll have a good holiday."

"That's not the point. Easter is the main celebration of the year in church. Besides, I get to be a reader for the first time."

"I'm sure they would excuse you." She made it sound as if I were planning to skip school.

"It's not a matter of being excused." I was floundering. How did I tell these nice people that I *wanted* to go to church and to be a part of the celebration?

"Oh, I see." Eve lowered her voice. "You can't very well tell them you're not coming to church because you're going to Vegas. Let's see, you could say you were off on a charter flight and not tell them where."

"But…"

"Or you could say you were sick. Or aren't you supposed to tell lies to your minister?" Eve winked at Joyce, who grinned.

"I *want* to go to church. I *want* to be a reader. It's an honour. It is the most special time of year. And no, I won't lie to my priest."

Ralph smoothed his receding grey hair and looked solemn. "I suppose Easter is the one time of year a person does have to show up in church. That and Christmas. I can remember getting dragged off to church those two days when I was a kid."

"This isn't the one time of year I go to church. I go every week. But Easter, in fact all of Holy Week, is a special time. I don't want to miss any of it." I liked Eve and Ralph, but they were getting on my nerves. They had put me on the defensive. Since I was as yet unsure in my faith, glib answers didn't flow readily from my lips. As I tended to do when cornered, I became aggressive. "I can't go. Period. I'm going to celebrate Easter at my church."

Immediately I regretted my words. I could see from their crestfallen expressions that their buoyant mood of a moment before had been punctured. Ralph and Eve showed the dismay of rejection by someone they liked. Joyce's face registered shock that I would treat one of my best customers in that way. I felt like sneaking a peek at my feet to see if they had turned to clay. I could feel my face flame red with embarrassment and anger at myself.

"I'm sorry," I stammered. "But I really do value my church association, and this is a special time of year that I don't want to miss. I'll let another instructor go, though, and you can do your instrument flying."

They were only slightly mollified. "We wanted you to go with us. Maybe another time." From Eve's stony tone of voice, I knew there would not be another time.

After the Thompsons marched out the door, Terry cornered me. Like a puppy begging for affection, he asked, "D'you think you could talk them into taking *me* with them? I'd *love* to make a trip like that!"

A faint smile twisted my lips.

"I'll see what I can do. Give them a bit of time to get over their disappointment, then I'll call them and suggest it. I'll put it on the basis of you're needing the experience." This was true. Terry yearned to be an airline pilot. This required hours and hours of flying experience, and a long-distance instrument instructional flight in a twin would look a lot better in his logbook than a dozen flights doing circuits and bumps. I usually didn't hire young instructors who wanted to use their job to build up hours so they could get on with the airlines. I wanted professional instructors, ones who wanted to teach flying because they loved doing just that. Terry, however, had been a student here, and had shown that he would do any job to the very best of his ability. He took instructing seriously and was good at it. I had never regretted the decision to hire him.

Terry's dark, handsome face, topped by black hair neatly and expensively waved in a style meant to look casual, lit up. He gave me the smile that had all the girls around the place swooning and said fervently, "Thanks. I sure appreciate that. Lay it on thick, will you?"

"Right you are, lover boy. Leave it to me."

Terry went into the pilot lounge, whistling a jaunty tune, visions of flights to Las Vegas in his head.

"I hope they'll let Terry fly with them," Joyce said wistfully.

"I do too."

"Do you really think that going to church is more important that taking a trip like that?"

"Yes."

Joyce shrugged. "I wouldn't, even if I wasn't getting paid for it. I'd grab at the chance. And to get paid for having fun, that would be great."

"Do you go to church at all?"

"Only at Christmas. I go to the United Church then."

"You're missing a lot."

Joyce merely shrugged again and went back to her work, obviously not wanting to talk about it. Damn! I thought. How do you talk to people about church or God? There used to be a time, most of my life in fact, when I would have responded in the same way. When anyone started talking to me about religion, I turned off my mind and headed toward the exit. How could I get around that attitude now that the shoe was on the other foot?

I had undergone a conversion experience only the previous summer, having just met Douglas Forsythe, our priest, and having found myself in a situation where I worked closely with him. He'd had the ability to understand what I needed and to answer my questions about the Christian faith in pithy, exciting explanations that stirred my interest. One day I quietly realized that I believed, where the previous day I hadn't. I couldn't put my finger on the exact moment of change or the reason for it. Douglas would probably have said that God chose His time to put it in my mind.

I was reminded of the opening of the Book of Jeremiah: "Then the Lord put out his hand and touched my mouth; and the Lord said to me, 'Now I have put my words in your mouth.'" Had the Lord reached out and touched my mind and put thoughts into it?

I seemed to be having a lot of trouble with my faith lately, I thought as I returned to my desk and listlessly tackled a pile of correspondence. It was like driving on the muddy or snow-covered roads in northern Alberta where I grew up. You spun your wheels a lot but never got anywhere very fast. And occasionally you slid sideways into the ditch. If I had analyzed my situation more carefully, I would have realized it was not my faith I was having trouble with, but my personal relationships. My problems were only beginning. Things were about to get worse.

THREE

The gloomy day dragged on like a Mahler symphony. Gayla had replaced Joyce, and was diligently and silently updating the student files. Through the open door of my office, I was vaguely aware of someone stopping in front of her desk and saying, with a bit of bluster in his voice, "I'd like to fly."

Gayla looked up in surprise. Instead of a quick and welcoming reply, she seemed at a loss for words. This caught my attention, so I dropped the aviation magazine I had been leafing through and walked toward the reception area, pausing in the doorway.

There stood the last person in the flying fraternity that I would have expected to see in my place of business. Lance Brock was not in my good graces. Last summer, he had brought a plane back late and lied to me about it. He had, I was told by another flight school owner, landed on an unlighted runway at night, a violation of the aviation regulations. On another occasion, I had caught him riding in the baggage compartment of a Cessna 152 belonging to the flying club at the other end of the field. This put the plane significantly over maximum allowable gross weight and way out of aerodynamic balance. At the same time, the 152 was being flown by an unlicensed young woman who was being taught to fly by her boyfriend, a teenager who had just gotten his private pilot license. To cap it all off, they'd had two six packs of beer on board. I had reported them, and Lance and the other young man had received reprimands from the Ministry of Transport. It could have been worse. The pilot could have had his license suspended.

I hadn't seen Lance since, and expected him to be angry with me. I had debated whether to let him fly at my school any more. My initial decision had been that if he asked, I'd give him another chance, provided he was willing to undergo refresher training. He had not asked, and eventually I'd forgotten about him. Now, here he was, his long thin face registering both belligerence and defensiveness.

"I want to fly," he repeated, his chin thrust forward and his fists jammed into the pockets of his flight jacket.

"Not today," I answered, walking over to the counter. The miserable day had at least one attribute: it allowed me to put off the final decision on whether to let Lance rent my planes. I didn't like his attitude. My magnanimous view that I should give him another chance, made last year at a time I was not standing face to face with him, now struck me as overly charitable.

He lowered his head, but his eyes flicked up in a quick glance at my face. "It's VFR," he muttered, but his voice lacked conviction.

"Maybe. When it rains, it socks in and you can't see halfway down the runway."

"I'm not chicken. A little rain doesn't bother me." The bluster was coming back.

"That's your trouble. Just because Visual Flight Rules are in effect at this particular moment doesn't mean that it's safe to fly. Especially not in these mountains." Our little city of Exeter is set in a mountain valley, beside long, fjord-like Lake Devon. Mountain ranges rise steeply on both sides, and on days like this, more than half their height is obscured in thick, grey cloud.

"I could stay in the valley."

"If," I stressed, "you could see where the valley was. Even experienced pilots know that conditions like we have today are an invitation to disaster, and stay on the ground."

Lance deflated like a day-old balloon. "Shit! The club plane is in the shop and I don't have anything to fly."

"Then consider yourself fortunate."

He glared at me. "What's that supposed to mean?"

I took a deep breath. "Lance, before you can fly here, you will have to undergo some extensive retraining, especially ground school on the regs, weather and flight planning. Your card is in the file of pilots who are not allowed to fly solo, so don't try to sneak in here behind my back. No one is going to rent you an airplane."

"Yeah, I know. I tried it yesterday."

I nearly erupted like Mt. Vesuvius, but with difficulty controlled my temper. Lance took one look at my red face, angry green eyes and fiery hair and decided not to push his luck. He slithered out the door, just as the next shower dumped its load and sent him scampering to his vehicle.

Lance hadn't changed, I realized. This re-opened my concern about whether I should give him another chance — presuming he asked. He would find someplace to fly, I knew, and perhaps it would be better if he did it here, where I could keep my eye on him and ascertain that he conformed to the regulations and to good flying practices. I could do as I did with student pilots after they have soloed. Their card in the school files is tagged with an orange marker, which indicated that some special provision to their solo flying was in effect. With students, this provision was that they must get the approval of an instructor before flying.

A red tag meant that the pilot could not fly solo, but must go up with an instructor. This applied to pre-solo students as well as problem pilots. Lance was definitely a red-tag pilot.

He had always been a problem for us. He hadn't crossed our threshold in the normal fashion: learn to fly, then buy an airplane, or continue to rent our planes. He had bought a plane first; an aerobatic, tail-wheel Citabria, and had then come in to get flying lessons. I had seen the Citabria over the previous two or three weeks, being flown in an erratic fashion. Lance's buddy, from whom he had bought a part interest in the plane, was attempting to teach him how to fly it. On their first "lesson" they did aerobatics! Lance had since done enough takeoffs and landings that he and his buddy felt he could fly it without total disaster.

They had been performing these controlled crashes over at Pine Hill, where they didn't have to contend with a control tower. Having to deal with Air Traffic Control is a distraction to beginning students, even when flying with experienced instructors.

Furthermore, the controllers might detect the unauthorized nature of their activity and report them. While they were taking a coffee break at the little hole-in-the-wall cafe that was an institution in these parts, the local flight school operator, Garth Hughes, had taken the opportunity to impart some of his aviation wisdom. The two young men didn't know who Garth was, so were willing to talk to him. He quietly drew out the whole story.

Garth then informed Lance that before he could go solo, he would have to obtain a student pilot license, pass a medical exam, and receive approval from a flight instructor of Class Three or above, or at least have his authorization to solo countersigned by one if he flew with a Class Four instructor. When Lance proposed to "skip all that crap," Garth had told him who he was and threatened both the young men with legal mayhem if they did any more "flight training." Garth did not want them at his school; Lance had come to mine.

His first appearance in my office had been similar to today's. He arrived carrying a chip as large as the tail of a C130 Hercules on his shoulder, pouting about the old creep over at Pine Hill, and telling (not asking, telling!) me that he wanted to hire an instructor to solo him. I had silently blasted "the old creep over at Pine Hill" for dumping his problem baby off onto me. Garth Hughes and I at that time treated each other like two tomcats meeting in the same back yard. This attitude dated back to the days when my ex, Dale Carruthers, ran the school and had a nice little sideline in stealing everyone else's business. Garth, it seemed, was now giving me some business, some that I wanted as much as I'd want an engine failure at 500 feet while flying down a boulder-strewn canyon.

I had itemized with Lance what my requirements were for flying with a student who owned his own plane. They were pretty strict. He'd have to park the Citabria at the school, and leave the keys with us. He would have the same restrictions on his flying as any other student pilot. His plane would be subjected to the same maintenance standards as our own, which would include an initial inspection by our maintenance chief, Rod O'Donnell, at Lance's expense. Any discrepancies would have to be remedied. Lance would be required to attend ground school and start at the beginning of the curriculum. He had stomped away, fuming.

He'd returned, though, his pride dragging like a scolded puppy's tail, because no one else would take him on. I had been the only one willing to work with him. He knew that if he continued to fly without a license, someone would report him.

I assigned him to my chief flight instructor, "Ace" Flynn. Ace had carried that well-deserved moniker ever since he had started to fly in his teens. His real name was Harold, but hardly anyone knew it. Ace was an old-timer, now retired, who had learned his flying in taildraggers and had taught many a young smart-ass back in the old days when flight training was a lot less structured.

Ace had made a world of difference in Lance's attitude, as well as in his aptitude. I didn't ask Ace for an accounting, and I suspect Ace used the threat method to advantage. Lance was one student, I realized, where that approach might work. At any rate, several months later, a thoroughly housebroken Lance came meekly to me for his flight test. He didn't excel, but he didn't just scrape by either. That was about two years ago.

Since then, Lance's buddy had pranged the Citabria. It was damaged beyond affordable fixing, and they hadn't bothered insuring it. They sold it for salvage and Lance started renting our Cessnas. I required him to have a check-ride every six months. He'd passed them and I'd warily rented him my planes — until that time last summer.

In the nine months since, during which time he continued to fly the beat-up old orange Cessna 152 belonging to the flying club, instead of becoming more expert with practice, he'd "gotten behind the power curve," his skill eroding with time. He needed a good kick in the pants, as well as many hours of dual instruction. I felt more concerned than ever that if he continued on his own, he would cause a serious accident, perhaps killing people, not to mention creating volumes of adverse publicity for aviation. Should

I call him, try to talk him into taking a refresher course? Persuade him to work with us to elevate his flying skills to an acceptable level?

I reached for the phone, then hesitated, my hand poised above the receiver. I really didn't want to have anything more to do with Lance Brock. Conscience and personal aversion stalemated. I dialled Ralph and Eve instead. They were at first frosty to my suggestion that they take Terry McGregor with them to Las Vegas, but soon warmed to the idea. "Terry needs the experience," I explained. "He would be good company, and he's a very good instructor."

"Oh, that would be fine," Eve replied. "He's a nice boy." I could sense the smile as she said it. Terry is adept at winning over the ladies — of any age. She didn't even sound disappointed that I wasn't coming, I noted, more piqued than I'd a right to be.

I sought out Terry and gave him the good news. He was elated.

As it turned out, I didn't have to call Lance. The next day he returned, quiet and polite. He had a suggestion. "I think I'd like to work on my commercial license. When can I start?"

It may be a face-saving gesture, I thought, but as long as he is serious, is willing to follow the rules, I'll go along.

My two most experienced instructors were Terry and Jan van den Bergh, my only female instructor. Lance Brock might make mincemeat out of Jan. She was very good with female students and teenagers, but got frustrated by older men who tried to tell her what they would and wouldn't do. The choice was obvious.

"I'll have you fly with Terry McGregor," I announced, "but he's going on a long charter this weekend and won't be back for a week. You can get your supplies and begin studying. We'll start with ground school. If the weather breaks, I'll fly with you until Terry gets back."

"Okay."

27

"Or, I could see if Ace Flynn will be available to fly just with you."

Lance shuddered. "No, no," he replied quickly. "I'll fly with you and Terry."

I bent over the papers on my desk to hide my smirk.

Wednesday of Holy Week was another washout for flying. Tuesday's showers had turned into Wednesday's cold drizzle. The overcast hung in sodden heaps along the valley. Forested mountains rose darkly toward the louring clouds and disappeared, their tops sheathed in the enveloping grey. I slept in late, then went to the early morning Eucharist being held at the church each Wednesday in Lent.

Only half a dozen bleary-eyed parishioners sat languidly in the pews nearest the altar, a huddled cluster of rain-coated humanity. Red, signifying blood, had replaced the Lenten purple as the liturgical colour for most of the week. Two white candles, burned nearly down to their stubs, flickered on the altar. In the silence, each individual's breathing, interspersed by an occasional cough, could be clearly heard. Then the Reverend Douglas Forsythe walked in from the south side of the chancel, the rich red brocade of his chasuble catching the glittering lights. A rustle of clothing and scuffling of feet accompanied the rising of the congregation to its feet. Douglas stopped in front of the altar, turned to face us, and exclaimed in an exultant voice, "This is the day that the Lord has made. Let us rejoice and be glad in it." Suddenly, the darkness seemed dispelled, the mood lightened, and we looked with anticipation to the coming Eucharist.

Douglas did that to us! I had always thought it incredible that by his presence and by a few words of scripture, he could change the countenance of our little corner of creation.

The older parishioners knew the *Prayer Book* by heart, and didn't bother opening it. I, on the other hand, had finally become comfortable with the new *Book of Alternative Services*, and had trouble keeping up with the *Prayer Book* service. I fumbled through

28

the pages, coming in about three words late in all the responses. Someday I'd learn it, I told myself.

Douglas' homily was the last one in a Lenten series that had sometimes gently chided, at others more vigorously exhorted us to follow in the footsteps of Christ; had reminded us that forces of evil constantly whisper in our ear or lure us with fanfare to "enjoy life" and abandon our Christian ways. We were to resist these evil forces, to live in love and charity with our neighbours, to give alms, to do good works, and when we had sinned, to repent and return to the Lord. Nothing new. It was the way he could say it, with passionate belief that made the difference. Before I had met Douglas, I hadn't been able to swallow such dogma.

I led a pretty good life, I thought. I'd been honest and fair, tolerant toward people of other races or cultures, and had tried to set a good example in the things I did. I felt that the only time I had the right to do something nasty to anyone else was if they had first done it to me. If I had summed it up, I would have said, "If you have power over other people, be fair. If you don't, get even."

When I later tried to relate that attitude to Christian teaching, I found that it fell far short of the ideal. Christianity, with its emphasis on turning the other cheek, walking the extra mile and praying for those who persecute you, was a much more difficult path to travel. It took a conscious effort to live as Jesus would have commanded. Spiritually, I was constantly stumbling and falling. I was learning that all is not lost when one does stumble and fall. Forgiveness is never withheld if one seriously repents. Repentance, however, is not just muttering, "I'm sorry." It must be a sincere desire to change one's ways, to turn one's life around and follow the Lord. And although I did humbly repent, I kept tripping time after time. Would I ever learn?

My Christian growth seemed to be at a standstill. Yes, I decided, I really had to talk to Douglas. Instead of my usual habit of immediately leaving the church after the service, I turned my footsteps toward the church office. That simple act propelled me into the relentless vortex of events that would unfold.

FOUR

When there were only a few of us, as at this service, we usually left by a door on the south side near the front of the nave. This brought us into a corridor that led to the church offices. I had hoped to catch Douglas as he went into his office to remove his vestments. As I stepped into the corridor, however, I could see Douglas at the far end and over his shoulder I saw the carefully coifed white head of Faith LaBounty. She had not been in the church and I wondered what she was doing there. Then I heard the booming Australian accents of Clive Hawthorne greeting Douglas, Paul and Owen who were ahead of me.

"Good morning mates." He made it sound like "mites."

"Good morning," the men chorused cheerfully. They stood in a group, exchanging greetings, and as I approached, I was suctioned into the tight little knot of chatting folk. I eyed Clive, still feeling suspicious of his interest in Faith. In spite of the weather, Clive was dressed for tennis: white shorts and a patterned jersey, open at the neck. He looked muscular and virile — and his thick chest hair was white. I glanced at his head of sandy hair, each strand perfectly in place. It was so expertly done, unless you looked especially closely, you couldn't tell that it was a wig. Nor that his eyebrows were dyed, but dyed they must have been. They were the same sandy colour as his hair. Not a strand of white anywhere, yet the hair on his head must be at least partially white for his body hair to be completely so.

Faith attached herself to me. "Robin, isn't it wonderful! Clive and I are going to be married."

As a conversation stopper, it was a corker! Eyes wide as alms basins, everyone stared at her in disbelief.

"Well, well, well!" Douglas exclaimed. "That's wonderful. Come on in."

Faith squeezed my hand. I was too dumbfounded to respond. She followed Douglas into the office, with Clive bringing up the rear. The door closed. So much for my plan to ask Douglas for a counselling session this morning.

"I would never have believed it," Paul murmured. "I think they must have met only within the last week or two."

"Since the next to last bible study two weeks ago Monday," I responded. "She was her usual mousy self at that time, and I drove her home. There weren't any boyfriends lurking on her doorstep. I waited until she had unlocked the door and turned on the interior lights before I drove away."

"Perhaps they knew each other somewhere before," Owen suggested.

"Could be. You never would have known it, though," Paul agreed. "Well anyway, he seems a nice enough chap." Paul's face had a wistful expression and I suspected that he was thinking of Penny, more than thirty years his junior, with whom he seemed to be infatuated. Penny treated Paul like a favourite uncle, but Paul's idolization of that young woman was definitely not so platonic.

Owen echoed Paul's sentiment. "Yes indeed. I'm happy for our little Faith. She seemed so lonely."

Was I the only person in all of Exeter who didn't like Clive Hawthorne?

Paul said good-bye and went on his way, leaving me with Owen. Not the company I would choose to be stuck with. He reminded me, "I'm doing Compline Sunday night. You'll be there won't you?"

"I thought it would be cancelled because Douglas is taking some time off, so I made other plans," I lied, sinner that I am. Chicken, I told myself.

Owen sounded disappointed. "I hope someone will come. Paul told me he is leaving for a trip to the UK after church on Sunday. That only leaves the Meachams and Miss Farnham of the regulars."

"Penny is going with me, so she won't be there, but I expect that some of the others will."

"I'm going on a trip myself. I was going to leave Sunday afternoon, but I felt that I should make myself available to take Compline, since I've had experience."

"Where are you going?" I asked, more out of tact than any real interest.

"I'm making a sales trip to Alberta; to Calgary and Edmonton mainly. My business is mainly clustered around areas where I was known before — southern Ontario and Nova Scotia as well as Vancouver and the BC interior. It has spread a bit from those areas. I have some clients in Quebec, around Hull, and in New Brunswick. I want to move into the Montreal market, and am planning to hit that area this summer. First, I'm working across the prairies."

I knew that Owen was an accountant, and wondered how he could sell his services so widely. I asked him.

"Computers my dear, computers. And all the wonderful gadgets that go with them. Do you know much about computers?"

"Not much. Airplanes are more my thing."

"I'm surprised they're not computerized."

"Navigation systems are these days. I personally don't totally trust them, but we use GPS — global positioning satellite receivers — in our more sophisticated planes, and that's run by computers. It's pretty useful. But I mainly teach flying. I have to train pilots that can navigate by the old-fashioned methods as well as the new. They can pick up all the fancy stuff later on."

"You teach dead reckoning?" asked Owen, referring to an ancient method of navigating that uses mathematical calculations of time, distance, ground speed and wind drift.

"You bet! That and pilotage — map reading — are the mainstays of navigation. If your radios fail or your electrical system goes out, that's what you have to rely on. I teach our students to always have a heading in mind, even if they're only going to the practice area. If the weather deteriorates and they can't see the airport, they can take the reciprocal of the heading they flew out on and have one to take them back."

"Sounds like a good idea. I once thought I'd like to learn to fly, but I never got around to it."

Just as well, I thought. It might be difficult to blast open his rigid mind-set in order to insert new ideas. People like that don't make good pilots. Yet he seemed to have modern ideas about accounting procedures. He hadn't impressed me as a person who'd be comfortable with computers, but apparently he was.

Owen launched into a description of how his computerized accounting system worked. "What you can do with the Internet is a revolution. I can sit here in Exeter and do the books for a firm in Halifax and get the results done faster than if they hired a bookkeeper to do it. I'm after a niche market. Small companies, especially those run by highly trained technical people who really don't know business as such. Engineers, for example. They have an idea that they can manufacture a product that will fill a need. I've got one client who runs a company that does nothing but bend tubing; not manufacture it, just bend it. Mind you, it's very sophisticated stuff that has to be very precise. Some of these boys are regular whiz kids at the engineering end of things, but they don't know how to run a business. The next person they hire is a high-powered salesman. Then they hire someone off the street to do their books. When they get themselves in a complete mess, I can sell them on my system. Some of them don't need a full-time bookkeeper. They only have to use me when they need me. I can do the work for a fraction of what they'd have to pay to hire a competent person, and in far less time than if they sent it out to an accounting firm of the usual type."

"I don't know about that. My accountant gives me really good service, and she knows aviation. Her husband, who is a lawyer, took lessons from us about ten years ago. She became very enthusiastic about flying as well. They fly nearly everywhere they want to go. I was just getting to the point where I couldn't handle the books myself, and I asked her advice. She's done a wonderful job for me."

"Would that be Ginny Meredith?"

"That's right."

"Ah, yes. She's quite good. You're lucky. I guess I won't get your business."

"No. I'm very happy with Ginny. Are you just going to Alberta and hope you find someone who needs you, or do you have some method of searching them out?"

"Of course I have. I do market research. I send out flyers and when a company responds, I set up an appointment with them. I also advertise on the Internet. I've got quite a list of prospects lined up."

"How do you find these companies?"

"Various ways. When I started, I knew from my own experience as the chief accountant at several big firms, that there were smaller companies supplying their products to us, whose accounting practices made me tear my hair out. There seemed to be a crying need for the kind of service I provide, and if I say so myself, I've been very successful. The business is growing like weeds in a garden." Frankly, he didn't look that successful. He was dressed that morning in an old plaid flannel shirt, baggy cords and a battered-looking windbreaker. I knew that he lived in a duplex that must have been built thirty years ago, making it old by Exeter's standards, and that he drove a five-year-old Ford Escort.

"That's excellent." I said. "But you must have to hire a lot of expert accountants."

"I don't have to hire any!"

"But…" My forehead knotted into a frown, wondering how he could do all the bookkeeping, and the sales work, by himself.

Owen laughed, showing white dentures in his craggy, weather-beaten face, topped by unruly grey hair. "Actually, I have one, Elliot Truesdale, who runs the place when I'm not there and can handle anything that comes along. Then I hire very competent computer people, ones who are conscientious about absolute accuracy. They do the work. Everything is on the computer programs. They just have to enter the data. I pay them well, but not as much as I'd have to pay a stable of chartered accountants."

"What do you do yourself, other than selling your services to new customers?"

"I oversee everything. I check up on the work being done. When a firm has had problems, I keep a close eye on them. I watch to see that we are doing what they need, and that they send us the data we require in a timely fashion. I keep my finger on everything. I'm the trouble-shooter. Elliot Truesdale runs the office."

In a lull in the conversation, I remembered Owen's reference to the Yukon. "When did you live in Kluane Junction? Surely you weren't an accountant for some big business up there."

Owen laughed. "You'd be surprised," he said. "Actually, what happened was that I got sick and my brother, who is in mining, suggested that I stay with him while I recuperated. He operates out of Kluane Junction and has several mines up there in the Yukon. His was just the kind of company I've been talking about. He'd hired the wife of one of his mine managers to do the books. Just before I came, he'd begun to have doubts about her. He didn't say anything to me until he was sure I was well and had my strength back. Then he confided in me, and because I was the boss's brother and supposedly just hanging around, I could poke my nose into everything.

"Well, let me tell you! That lady was stealing my brother blind! I very quietly got all the evidence together, then he got the RCMP in there so fast, she hadn't a chance to dispose of anything or erase anything on the computer. My brother had to fire the mine manager as well; man by the name of Sam Kruse. Kruse raised a stink, but my brother was well thought of, and the evidence of embezzlement was so compelling, that everyone sided with my brother. Kruse finally left town.

"Then, while I was still in the Yukon, my old boss back in Toronto had some problems that I was able to work out for him with material he sent me by fax. With all this fancy new stuff you can do with computers, it was like sitting at a table and going over the books with him. So it gave me the idea of starting an accounting business, using computers, and hitting this niche market of small businesses."

"I see." My impression of Owen had unexpectedly gained altitude.

"Yes, it's working out well."

"That's good. Well, I wish you success on your sales trip."

"I expect that I shall have it It's not hard to sell a good product." There was a smug purr to his voice.

When I arrived at Red Robin Flying School, the first people I saw were Ginny and Wilf Meredith.

"We're hoping the weather will clear so we can fly to Georgetown over the holiday weekend," Wilf explained. "The forecast is encouraging. They call for gradual clearing over the next two days. Maybe by Friday it will be good enough. Do you have a Cessna 172 available?"

"Let's look." I opened the schedule book to the appropriate page. "When would you be back?"

"Sunday evening, weather permitting. We'd want to stay until the hunt is over."

I must have looked perplexed. "Easter egg hunt," Ginny reminded me. "It's Easter."

"I know it's Easter, but I think of Easter in terms of church, not eggs and bunnies."

"That's what comes of not having children," Ginny, who had two, stated knowingly, laughter in her voice. "What about a plane?"

"Both planes are scheduled at some time during the weekend, but there's no overlap, so I can move a couple of students out of Five into Four. Neither of them has to have Five." We designated our planes by a number displayed prominently on the tail. The trainers, three Cessna 150s, were called Robin 1, Robin 2 and Robin 3. The two 172s, small four-place planes, were Robin

4 and Robin 5. The sixth plane in the fleet, a Beech A36 Bonanza used in charter work, was seldom referred to by a number and did not have one on it's tail. All the planes were painted red and white and carried a logo composed of a chirpy little red bird plus the name of the school. My own personal airplane was a retired military trainer; a bright yellow, fully aerobatic deHaviland Chipmunk taildragger. It was seldom used for training at the school.

I transferred the two students who had been scheduled in Robin 5 into Robin 4 and scheduled the Merediths in Robin 5 for the holiday weekend. This was our instrument trainer, and was equipped with all the navigation radios needed for flying by instruments. It sported a new GPS receiver and was favoured by pilots making long cross-country flights. I had no qualms about Wilf. He would be careful about the weather, which I hoped would be cooperative for their trip.

"We'll see you out here Friday morning," Ginny said.

"No. I won't be here. I'll be in church. It's Good Friday."

She eyed me quizzically. "You don't look like the kind of person who would go to church." She made it sound distasteful. Should I turn green or sprout some weird appendage? Why should a church-goer look different?

"Why not? No one in the church seems particularly unusual as far as I can see."

"It's just that you expect them to be kind of nutty." Her voice held a hint of sarcasm.

"Where did you get that idea?" I inquired defensively.

Ginny shrugged and shifted her weight from one foot to the other in embarrassment.

"Do you really believe in God?" Wilf asked.

"Yes, I do."

"I can't imagine any old man sitting up on the clouds, myself."

"Neither can I, and I doubt if there's a single person in our church who does." The defensiveness was still there in my voice.

"Well, you can have your church. I'd rather be flying."

I didn't know how to answer that. I don't think I could survive without my regular flying "fix." Flying has consumed most of my adult life, and the thrill has yet to wane. Was it only because the planes would still be there to fly when I came back that I was willing to give up flying in order to go to church?

Finally Ginny broke the lengthening silence. "Anything I need to do on the financial front before I leave?"

"Not that I can think of. By the way, do you know Owen Dunphy?"

"Yes, I know him."

"What's your opinion of this business of his?"

"Top rate. I wish I'd thought of it. But then, I wouldn't have had the money and the connections, to say nothing of the nerve, to start something like that. He had a good idea at the right time and cashed in on it."

"Is he doing well?"

"He's probably swimming in money. I've never seen anything take off like that did. You aren't thinking of switching are you?"

"Oh no," I assured her hastily. "I saw him in church this morning and we stopped to talk. His business is beyond my comprehension."

"I dare say yours is beyond his comprehension, too."

"I doubt it. I thoroughly expect him to start telling me how to fly any day."

Ginny shrieked with laughter. "Knowing Owen, I expect that he might."

Lance Brock had also gotten the forecast of improving weather and called to make an appointment for the following day. Joyce and Gayla had rounded up several pilots who were interested in ground school for the commercial pilot license. A course was scheduled. Jan was designated as the instructor. She was an excellent ground school teacher, and brought a vivid imagination to the job. Her courses were never dull. I called Ace Flynn to ask him to teach the part on bush flying, as many commercial pilots end up in that sort of job. I didn't tell him that Lance was to be one of the students. Chicken, again!

Terry McGregor did a good imitation of walking on air as he contemplated his upcoming trip. Ralph could be seen polishing the Twin Comanche while Eve sat in the pilots' lounge plotting courses.

"You'd better let Ralph do that," I told her. "If he's taking instrument instruction, he needs to do his flight planning himself."

"He's doing that," Eve replied, her eyes behind thick-lensed glasses twinkling. "But I want to be able to follow along myself. This is for me."

"Good. I hope you enjoy your trip and hit the jackpot in the casinos."

"If we do, Ralph will just spend it on a bigger, fancier airplane."

I left the airport at about four fifteen and drove to the church. Douglas was ensconced in his office with a young couple whose baby was to be baptized, so I sat down to wait. It was about twenty to five when they came out of the office. They stood around talking for a few minutes, then left, and Douglas turned to me, a welcoming smile on his finely chiselled face.

"What brings you here?" he asked.

"I'd like a few minutes sometime to talk to you. I know you're busy right now with Easter and you'll be away next week, but any time after that if you have some time, I'd appreciate it."

"Why don't you come in right now?" He gestured toward the office. "There is no meeting to go to this evening, for once, and I'm not in a hurry to get home and have dinner since I don't have to run off again."

"But Betty's probably waiting for you."

"I'll call her and tell her I'll be home in a short while." Douglas picked up the phone and dialled the rectory number.

"Hello dear. I'll be a bit late. Robin is here and has something to go over with me. What's that? Okay I'll ask."

He turned toward me. "Betty says for you to come to the house for dinner, and we can talk in my office there."

"I don't want to barge in on you."

I could hear the receiver make noises. Douglas grinned and handed it to me.

"I told that husband of mine that he was to drag you up here," said Betty Forsythe. "I've got a lovely pot roast, surrounded by luscious vegetables. There's enough to feed an army. Roasts are better if you get a big one. We haven't had you over for a while, anyway, so come on up."

"The pot roast did it! I'll come."

FIVE

Douglas reclined in an easy chair, his legs stretched out, ankles crossed, his hands folded across his waist, looking completely relaxed. He had removed his shoes, and I for once had remembered to do so when I had entered the house. Douglas slipped the white plastic clerical collar out of the neck of his black shirt and undid the top button. Of medium height and build, he still managed to keep his trim waistline. How he could do so with all the potluck dinners he had to attend in his role as parish priest was beyond me. There was more grey in his brown hair than there had been when I first met him nearly a year ago. His warm brown eyes still had the same twinkle, and the laugh lines at the corners of his eyes were evident. An ordinary-looking man, but something about him that I could not precisely define, radiated character.

Douglas had replaced a very popular priest who had retired because of illness. He had wowed us with his oratory, astonished us with his capacity for getting things done, and for me at least, had seemed able to look into my very soul. Had it not been for an unusual opportunity to work in close association with him, I might still be floating around on the periphery of the church, a non-believer.

His wife Betty, a bouncy, outgoing blonde with eyes the colour of a prairie sky, had been an immediate hit in the parish. Her mass of blonde curls and tinkling laugh were familiar at St. Matthew's Anglican Church, as she became active in groups ranging from the choir to the Altar Guild.

Through the living room window we could see a neighbour walking his Corgi dog. "Do you know anything about Corgis?" Douglas asked me. "We want to get a dog and I was wondering…"

"We're getting a cat," Betty stated emphatically, appearing from the kitchen, a ladle in her hand.

"A dog," he replied, teasing her.

"A cat!" Betty walked behind his chair on her way back to the kitchen and gave him a little swat on the back of his head as she passed.

"Robin, do you think the Rector of St. Matthew's should have to put up with this insubordination in his own rectory?"

"The rectory is my domain," Betty declared.

"Don't drag me into this," I protested. "I refuse to take sides."

Douglas leaned his head back so that he could see his wife as she worked in the kitchen and mouthed the word, "Dog."

Betty went through the motions of throwing something at him, made a face and spat back, "Cat." He grinned at her.

They were a pair, those two! Obviously still deeply in love after many years of marriage, they could, at times, act like young lovers. I had seen them walking down the street holding hands or hugging each other closely as they watched something they enjoyed. I envied them.

My own marriage had been brief, ill-conceived, and had soured me on the masculine half of the human race. Until last year, when I had met Douglas Forsythe, that is. I had, for a while, thought I'd fallen in love with him. Still, I could not imagine myself in this marriage. I was a career woman before everything else. I'd have to be on equal footing with any man I teamed up with. I was not designed to be a housewife or a mother. The thought of flocks of grandchildren coming to visit didn't fill me with visions of joy. The Forsythe's three children, the spouses of two of them, and three grandchildren had been present at Douglas' induction last summer, and even the big rectory must have been crammed full. I liked my peace and quiet, my solitude.

But occasionally I was lonely, and an invitation to share a meal with these comfortable people was welcome.

We sat down to a meal of tender beef roast, with carrots, onions, and small potatoes browned in the beef juices. Following the apple pie, served with a cinnamon sauce, Betty shooed us off to Douglas' office while she did the dishes.

Douglas made small talk for a few minutes, then looked at me questioningly.

"We haven't had a talk for a while. How are you getting along?" he asked.

"You crammed me so full of information last fall, I'm still digesting it."

"But now you've reached a sticking point. Is that right?"

"Yes." I gathered my thoughts, trying to decide how to begin. I smoothed down my red hair, then not knowing what to do with my hands, rubbed them together. "It's the reaction of people toward the church that bothers me." Douglas made a wry face. I wondered how he handled this problem, or if his clerical collar served to ward off the sceptical.

"We're constantly being told that we should spread the word, and I want to do so, but I seem to continually run into a brick wall. People aren't interested and they think I'm nuts." I told him about my recent experiences with Joyce, with Ralph and Eve, and Ginny and Wilf.

"That's a common experience," Douglas told me. "Don't let it get you down." Did I detect a note of resignation in his voice?

"Sometimes I feel like hiding the fact that I go to church and have accepted the Christian faith. I don't want to do that, but I'm chicken. I'm afraid of the way people will react."

"Let's take these people you're telling me about. First, your receptionist. You don't seriously believe that she thinks you're crazy, do you?"

"No. She just avoids talking about it."

"Which could be because she is unsure of herself, not because she thinks there is anything wrong with you. She may actually admire you for your courage in standing up for your faith. She would seem to be a believer, since she goes to church, if only once a year. She might be a person who would welcome the opportunity to become more active. Why don't you invite her to come to church with you?"

"I don't know about that! She doesn't seem very interested."

"But have you asked?"

I couldn't look at him. "No," I replied meekly to some imaginary presence in the corner of the room.

"From what I have seen of those two ladies who work for you, the few times I've met them, I have the impression that they regard you quite highly. That is due, I'm sure, to the way you run the business and treat your employees, but I seriously doubt if your becoming a Christian has affected their attitude to you in an adverse way. If you act out your faith by trying to follow in Jesus' footsteps, they will eventually see that you are doing so, and that may open their eyes to the reality of God's grace. Christians need to live the type of life that reflects Christ's teaching in a positive way. Then people who observe this will be compelled to find out what it's all about."

I nodded thoughtfully, and Douglas went on, "Let's look at the couple who wanted you to fly them to Las Vegas."

I grimaced. "I didn't handle that very well."

"But in the long run, you didn't lose their business."

"No."

"They would have thought less of you if you had been willing to compromise your belief and pursue the almighty dollar."

"I doubt if they'd give it a second thought."

"You might be surprised. And the same with the other couple."

I shifted uncomfortably in my chair. "The problem is, I can put myself in their shoes. I used to think that way. I had the idea that in order to believe in God, you had to accept all this kooky stuff that the fundamentalists throw around, and I just couldn't swallow it. I kept my thoughts to myself, but what Wilf Meredith said is what I used to think."

"So perhaps you are doing him a service by showing him that such beliefs aren't necessary. If he and his wife, who think religious people are nutty, see that an eminently sane and competent person firmly believes in God and is willing to put her reputation on the line in order to proclaim God's word, it might give them cause to think that there's something to it.

"Also, Robin, remember that present-day Christians are not the first to have to fight against disbelief, apathy or even persecution. So don't give up the fight."

It sounded so sensible!

But I had another problem. "Actually, what I first came here this morning to talk to you about is on the opposite end of the scale. I've been going to Harry and Shirley's bible study group, and one person there is the perfect example of what kept me away from the church for most of my life."

"In what way?"

"He believes that every word of the King James Version was written by God, but he puts his own interpretation on everything. He is sexist and homophobic, and he doesn't let anyone else get a word in edgeways, let alone express an opinion."

"Owen?"

"Yes."

Douglas leaned back in his swivel chair and stretched his arms over his head. He heaved a deep sigh. "Owen is a biblical literalist. So are a lot of other people, many of them Anglicans, though that's not our official position. To my way of thinking, literalists have to have logic-tight compartments in their minds in order to believe what they do. But if you try to point out what you think are errors in their reasoning or contradictions in the *Bible*, they can just shut you out. And it often is very upsetting to them to have their beliefs challenged, so one must tread carefully. After all, there's no harm done if that's what they want to believe."

"I don't agree," I stated flatly. "It's what gives Wilf his ammunition, and what kept me out of church for years."

"It sometimes attracts people to church. They want the certainty of something absolute."

I frowned and rested my chin on my hand. I'm not getting my point across, I thought. "I'm afraid to speak out at our bible study sessions because I don't know all that much. But I see the *Bible* differently."

"How do you see it?" Douglas leaned forward, keen interest showing in the intensity of his scrutiny.

"I think that the *Bible* is a record of people's attempts to communicate with God, or vice versa, passed along orally for hundreds of years before being written down, and that it includes the cultural interpretations of the people to which the events first occurred and possibly the changes of interpretation given it by others who passed the stories along and those who finally wrote it down. I've been reading the early books of the *Old Testament*, the *Pentateuch*, and those contain over and over again the exhortation, 'Remember this and tell it to your children.' This was their story and it had to be told over and over again orally, in order to be passed from generation to generation. To make it memorable, I think people illustrated the bare facts with exciting stories that aren't necessarily factual, but tell some basic truth. Am I too far off base?"

"You go right to the head of the class in modern Christian Theology."

I stared at Douglas in disbelief.

Douglas, watching me closely, asked, "What is it that bothers you most about Owen?"

"I don't like the way he hijacks the Bible study. I go there to learn, but I spend two hours listening to him rant and rave. We have a study guide, but we don't get a chance to use it. I can study at home, but I'd like to be able to discuss things rationally with other people."

"Robin, don't be afraid to express yourself. You have as much right to your view as the next person has to theirs. The Bible study is supposed to be for the purpose of exploring those views. The other members may be interested in what you have to say."

"But they know so much more than I do."

"Don't be so sure. Have you ever asked them why they come?"

"No."

"It is probably because they don't feel they know the Bible very well and want to learn more, just as you do. Perhaps none of them feel competent to argue with Owen. Owen is very sure of himself. He has his version of theology firmly fixed in his mind. He can produce a logical sequence of arguments for his position. I often don't agree with him, but I recognize that his version of theology is very standard and he can quote many highly regarded sources for corroboration. I can debate him because I feel confident of my position. You can debate him also, because you have a reasoned position from which to argue. Give it a try. The others may welcome having a champion for their cause."

"I generally tend to avoid arguing with people like that."

"You might find it challenging."

"All Owen wanted to talk about the other night was the subject of homosexuals. He can quote scripture but it isn't always accurate. Linda Meacham got on his case about that! Still, I know there are some Old Testament passages that disapprove of homosexuality, so I don't feel I can discuss it. I know that the Anglican Church is leaning in the direction of acceptance, and that the United Church has allowed the ordination of homosexuals. How can we square that with the scriptures?"

"Robin, go back to your description of how you see the Bible. You are in good company. There is a theology professor at Harvard who suggests that the early Israelite prohibition of homosexuality is based not on its immorality, but on the need for the small Israelite tribes to reproduce and multiply in order to survive in the face of hoards of adversaries.

"Also Robin, remember that times and attitudes changed over the centuries. In the days of Moses, the idea of 'an eye for an eye and a tooth for a tooth' was thought to be radically lenient. Yet it sounds barbaric in comparison with Christ's message of forgiveness. In the days of Moses, when a member of one tribe

47

injured a member of another, the kinsmen of the injured man would try to wipe out the offender's tribe, killing its men and taking its women.

"By the time of St. Paul, Christians were being told 'Bless those who persecute you; do not return evil for evil; do not avenge, but leave room for the wrath of God.' That's from Romans 12, by the way."

I thought it over for a few moments, and Douglas must have seen my morose expression. He continued, "And Robin, don't judge Owen entirely on his biblical interpretation. There are many people whose thinking is forward and up-to-date in everyday affairs, who still shut their minds off to any challenge to their religious beliefs. They are comfortable with what they believe and don't want to be changed. Who is your leader? Harry?"

"Yes, supposedly. But he can't control Owen. Owen runs the show. Penny is thinking of dropping out also."

"Hmm. I think I'll have to put in an appearance. When do you meet next?"

I gave him the date and he wrote it on his desk calendar. He said thoughtfully, "I have the responsibility for the overall supervision of Christian education in the parish. I need to be sure we are adhering to Anglican doctrine. I'll be at the next meeting. In the meantime, Robin, don't drop out. Stick with it. The group needs your perspective. You have something fresh to bring to it. Just don't expect everyone to agree with you."

As things turned out, I needn't have worried about how to handle Owen. I would never have another opportunity to confront him.

Back in the living room of the rectory, Betty came to join us, slipping off her sandals and tucking her feet under her as she nestled into the corner of the couch.

"I hear that Faith LaBounty is going to marry some fellow from Australia," she commented. "When is the big event to take place?"

Douglas gave a date for a Saturday later in the month.

"Faith of all people. Who would have believed it?"

"None of us." The Forsythes caught the contentious tone in my voice and stared at me for a moment before Douglas asked cautiously, "Is something wrong?"

"I'm just not excited about it. There's something about Clive that makes me uneasy for Faith's sake. I think he's a fake."

"What makes you think that?"

"He wears a wig and dyes his eyebrows. His hair is really white." It sounded pretty tame.

"Lots of people wear wigs. Don Urquhart does. He's bald as an onion."

"Yes, I know. I've seen him out at the farm. But he doesn't use it to hide under. It's grey, like the little fringe of real hair that he has. It matches his eyebrows. He's not faking anything."

"Except for the fact that he's bald."

I laughed. I could visualize Don Urquhart as I had first seen him in church. I'd thought he looked like a retired professor, one who'd occupied some endowed chair. When I heard that he ran The Veggie Farm, I couldn't believe it. I regularly went there to buy fresh fruits and vegetables, but had not connected the bald, T-shirted man hustling around with bins of veggies to the distinguished-looking man I had met in church. Don was not the usual small farmer or orchardist with a roadside stand. His business was big-time, renowned throughout the British Columbia Interior. He also had an interest in a frozen food processing plant. That plant's top line of quality vegetables and fruits came from Don's farm. In the church, Don served as a member of the Stewardship Committee, with the special role of "planned giving" coordinator, showing people how they could use their wills, their retirement accounts and other assets to benefit the church. The whole concept was beyond me, but I had heard that Don had been an insurance salesman before he had become a veggie farmer, had "burned out" and decided to go back to the land from whence he had come.

Scratching my head, I tried to put my thoughts into words. "Don is different. When he comes to church, he dresses up, the way a lot of older parishioners do. He puts on a good suit, and he puts on his hair. He's not really hiding the fact that he's bald, and he's not lying about his age. Clive is."

"Which is probably just a bit of vanity."

"Maybe. But there are other things. This hearty Australian mateyness seems contrived." I shrugged. "It's probably just my personal prejudice, but I hope he isn't after Faith's money. She appears to be pretty well-off."

Douglas sat quietly for a few minutes, stroking his chin. Then, in reasoned tones, he replied, "I have only met him the one time, this morning when he and Faith came to discuss wedding plans. He seemed very deferential and rather quiet. Faith did most of the talking. I didn't have much of a chance to evaluate him. I'm not actually going to marry them myself. Faith is a good friend of Olivia Marriott and wants Olivia to marry her. Olivia is quite popular with couples asking to be married, but she always sends them to ask if it is all right with me." Olivia Marriott was a retired priest, one of several who had moved to the mild climate and scenic beauty of Exeter on their retirement.

Betty entered the discussion. "I take it there are no impediments to their getting married in the church."

"No. They have both been married before and their spouses have died. Faith is a member of the church, of course, and Clive says he was baptized in the Anglican Church in Australia as a baby, but admits that he hasn't been a faithful church-goer."

"Divorced people can remarry, though, can't they?" I asked.

"Under certain conditions. A committee reviews the situation and makes a decision on whether a divorced person may remarry in the church. If you're one of these people who hop in and out of marriages like changing clothes, they are not going to approve it. But if you had good grounds for your divorce, and have given thoughtful consideration to your remarriage and appear to consider it a life-long commitment, then they will probably approve."

"You wouldn't be excommunicated if you went out and married several times in civil ceremonies, would you?"

"No. Not in our church. You would still be welcome as a member, even if you couldn't marry in the church."

A thought struck me. "There's a point in the service where you say that if there is anyone who has reason to believe that these people shouldn't be married, they should say so. Does that ever happen?"

Douglas had been gazing out the window. He turned his head sharply to look at me. His brow furrowed and he gave me a long, thoughtful look. "Yes. Why?"

"Oh, don't worry. I'm not going to get up and object in the middle of Faith's wedding. I doubt if I'll be there, anyway. Saturday is our busiest day. I was just curious."

I watched Douglas relax, the tension going out of his face, his body sinking back into the cushions of his chair. A smile crinkled the corners of his eyes and he chuckled. "I remember one time when I was a young priest and I married the prettiest girl in town to the lucky young man she had agreed to accept. All the other suitors were devastated, and one of them came to the wedding. He was quite drunk, but not so drunk that he couldn't follow the service, and sure enough, he got up and objected. He got quite vehement about it. I tried to placate him, to no avail, and finally he had to be ushered out. Do you remember that, Betty."

Betty's laugh danced across the room. "Do I ever! I also remember that the groom was about to flatten him and had to be restrained by the best man, and the bride had a hard time keeping from showing that she was enjoying it immensely."

That brought a flood of reminiscences about past weddings, with all the hilarious foibles, the ridiculous and the sublime. Finally Betty asked, "Why are Faith and her boyfriend getting married so soon? Aren't you supposed to counsel them?"

"About what, Dear? Am I supposed to tell them about the birds and the bees?" At which Betty threw a cushion at Douglas and the conversation about marriage came to an end.

I would put Faith and Clive out of my mind and let them do their thing, I decided. But that was not to be the end of my encounters with the problems of courtship, as I was soon to find out.

SIX

Late Thursday morning, I stood at the counter in the outer office reviewing the schedule when I heard a mellifluous voice address me.

"You must be Robin."

I glanced up and found myself looking into the face of a veritable Adonis, a man in his mid-twenties whom I can describe in no other term than "beautiful." "Handsome" wouldn't do it. I don't mean to imply that he seemed feminine. His beauty was definitely masculine; it was in the symmetry of his features, the smoothness of his skin, which should grace a commercial for shaving cream, the full lips and the widely spaced eyes of a vivid blue that I had seen previously only in Siamese cats. The face was topped by a head of golden curls that had recently seen an expert hairdresser. There was a friendly smile on the cherubic lips and a twinkle in the exotic eyes, underneath long, curved lashes.

I had never expected anything like that to walk into my place of business!

If he says he wants to learn how to fly, I thought, I'll fall over in a faint.

He did more than that. In his quiet, well-modulated voice, he said, "I want to get my commercial license. Dale said I should look you up."

Dale! My ex? Dale doesn't *know* people like this. Dale, if he saw this creature coming, would cross to the other side of the street. Dale, who taught me how to fly and from whom I acquired the flight school in our divorce settlement, was a bush pilot up north, flew fire bombers and hung around with the rough and ready outdoorsman type.

I finally got my mouth in working order and stammered, "Hi. Yes, I'm Robin. Where did you meet Dale?"

"In Whitehorse. He taught me to fly."

He taught *you* to fly? I asked myself. Dale doesn't teach flying any more, and I can't see him making an exception for you.

Adonis, seeming to realize that some explanation was indicated, continued. "My father has a engineering business in Whitehorse. Bridges are his thing, but he does other heavy construction as well. I'm a computer programmer. Actually, I devise programs. I've got copyrights on several of them, including one computer game. I did it several years ago when I was a teenager, but it's my biggest seller. I get really good royalties from it. Anyway, Dad wanted to upgrade his computers and asked me to come up and do it for him. He was a bit hesitant, because he'd been down to Vancouver a few times and seen me like this." He motioned toward his hairdo. "It didn't meet with parental approval, shall we say."

He paused for a moment to chuckle over the memory. "So when I went to Whitehorse, I let the old hair grow out then whacked off most of the curls. I dressed in jeans and stuff, so when I turned up in Whitehorse, Dad sort of recognized me." This day, he was dressed in neatly creased tan slacks, matching jacket, and a plaid wool shirt that had probably cost a bundle.

"It was in June, the days were 24 hours long, and I never got sleepy. I'd always wanted to learn to fly, and Dad's office faced the airport. I spent a lot of time watching planes come and go. Then I thought, what better time to learn to fly? You could fly all day and all night. So I went over to the airport and I ran into Dale. He said he didn't do much instructing any more, though he kept up his license, but he was sort of stuck there for a week, and he'd get me started.

"Well, I'd done all the ground school stuff about three times over. I wrote the exam and passed it, and I flew in every spare moment. As it turned out, Dale had to be there in Whitehorse for nearly two weeks and I managed to get through before he left. The next week, I passed my flight test. I had a great old time up there the rest of the summer."

"What type of plane did you learn in?"

"A guy there had a Super Cub that he rented to us, and I still had access to it after Dale left. Boy did I have fun!"

"Good. Dale is a top-notch instructor. If he taught you, and in a taildragger at that, I expect you know how to fly. Have you been keeping up during the winter?"

"Yeah. I was back in Vancouver, and I've been checked out in Cessnas and Cherokees. I fly every chance I get. The bug has definitely bit me, and I want to go on and learn more. I wrote to Dale and asked him who he would recommend. He said that if I could get away from Vancouver long enough, I should come up here. I don't know whether I'd want to be a commercial pilot as a steady job, but it seemed like a good way to get more proficient."

I agreed with that. I always try to get the pilots who fly at Red Robin to upgrade their skills. "We have a lot of other special courses here," I told him. "You name it and we can probably teach it to you."

"Right now, though, I've decided to go for the commercial. What do I have to do?"

"We're just starting a commercial ground school course tonight."

"Good. I'll be there."

Such eagerness to attend ground school was so rare as to be non-existent. Most students want nothing other than to get in an airplane and fly. They don't want to sit around in a classroom. I had been prepared for an argument, and this ready acceptance put me completely off my stride.

"You'll need the study materials. What's your name, by the way?"

"Oh, sorry. I didn't introduce myself. I'm Zane — Zane Rossiter." He held out his hand and when I took it, his handshake was firm and decisive.

"Okay Zane. Your ground school teacher is Jan. She's very good, but..." I stared intently at him, "...she's also very pretty. So

I want you to concentrate on the books and let her concentrate on her teaching."

He laughed delightedly, then straightened up and gave me a snappy military salute. "Yes Sir! I mean, yes Ma'am!"

"I never knew you made your students salute you," said a laughing voice from the end of the counter. I turned and saw Penny Farnham standing there. She wore a denim skirt and jacket and a checked cotton blouse. She had let her thick brown hair cascade over her shoulder. She sauntered over, eyeing Zane with more than casual interest. To me she said, "I'm on my way out to Three Lakes to give the school kiddies their needles, and I thought I'd see if you want to go to the airport restaurant for lunch."

"Is there a good restaurant on the field?" Zane asked, going over Penny's shapely figure with X-ray eyes.

"Yes, over on the other side, in the terminal," I responded.

"Well then, how would you ladies like to be my guests for lunch?"

I never turn down a luncheon invitation from a student, especially since most of my students are a lot more affluent than I am and can afford it. "Fine," I said.

"I'd be delighted." Penny looked as if she meant it.

As we entered the airport terminal, a deHaviland Dash 8, a small turboprop airliner designed for operation into mountain airports like ours, was disgorging its passengers. The arrival area was alive with seething humanity. A harried mother dragging three tired, whining children searched the crowd with anxious eyes. Finally recognizing a middle-aged couple pushing their way toward her, I could see her face relax and her body sag in the last stages of exhaustion. Rest, at last! The man gathered up her bags while the woman enfolded her in a welcoming embrace.

A slim blonde woman in her mid-thirties rushed into the arms of a tall, broad-shouldered man. Businessmen bustled toward the exit, briefcases in hand and raincoats slung over their arms. A family group looked anxiously toward the plane, the children jumping up and down or climbing onto the seats to get a better view. Finally, when all the other passengers had deplaned, a flight attendant helped an elderly woman negotiate the steps. The local agent had brought a wheelchair, but the old lady waved it away and turned to walk briskly toward the terminal, hardly using her cane, a look of excitement on her face.

"Here she comes! Here comes Gramma!" shouted the children, and the old lady disappeared into the enveloping presence of her welcoming family.

We walked on past the departure area. The people who were going out on the Dash 8 had already been herded into the holding pen and were now being let out to make a dash across the rain-splashed tarmac to the plane. A tired-looking man, obviously waiting for a later flight, slumped dejectedly in his seat. Another man was checking in, shoving a bulging suitcase through the opening under the counter. A young couple twined into a passionate embrace. I couldn't tell which one was going on the flight. In an out-of-the-way corner, a young mother inconspicuously breast-fed her baby.

We passed by all these people and climbed the stairs to the restaurant.

"Hi there, Robin," Sally, the waitress, called out from behind the coffee urn. "Sit anywhere you want."

We chose a table by the window, and Zane and I watched with professional interest as another Dash 8 broke off the instrument approach and manoeuvred onto the downwind leg of the circuit. We critiqued his approach and landing, which pilots are wont to do when they are hanging around an airport.

"Those planes can fly really slow, can't they? You could almost stay ahead of them in a 172," Zane remarked.

"They're made for operations in this kind of terrain," I explained, more for Penny's sake than Zane's. "This valley is fairly open, but when they have to go into some place like Castlegar, they have to be able to manoeuvre at slow speeds in tight spaces." Castlegar was down in a deep, narrow canyon, and if the landing had to be made toward the south, one had to make a ninety degree right turn onto short final after descending between towering mountains.

"I hear they used to go in there with 737s though," Zane remarked as we watched the Dash 8 touch down, sending up spray from the rain-soaked runway.

"That's right. I always thought they were pushing their luck a bit, but they seemed to do it okay."

"Do you have any jets come in here?"

"Yes. There's a morning and an evening flight each way using BAe 146s."

Penny watched us with amusement and remarked, "Now, you two. No shop talk."

"Okay," Zane readily agreed, diverting his attention from the outside world with alacrity. "You mentioned giving kids their needles. What kind of an ogre are you anyway?"

"I'm a public health nurse."

"Oh, I see. Do you take care of AIDS patients?"

"No. Someone else does that. My work is mainly with school children, giving them their immunizations, and teaching classes on health. I do some work with new mothers, also."

"Do you have children?" Zane had already checked out the ring finger on Penny's left hand. She wore no ring, no jewellery at all.

"Not I! Other people's kids are enough for me."

All through our meal, I watched Zane's smooth pick-up, and Penny's carefully calculated rear-guard action. She would not surrender easily. There was a man in her past life, one she never talked about, who must have had a devastating effect on her. She held most men at arm's length, but she was definitely interested in this one.

I left them to go back to my work. My last view showed them leaning toward each other across the table, smiling. Penny pushed a great mass of brown hair back from her face and Zane reached out to touch it. I was happy for Penny, but held a twinge of regret for Paul St. Cyr, who doted on her so.

Now why didn't this man, who had burst into our lives with the same suddenness that Clive Hawthorne had, bother me as Clive had done? Did I think Penny more capable of taking care of herself than Faith, or was it because Zane was a pilot and I liked pilots, especially ones who had learned their flying from Dale? I mentally shrugged off the question. Nothing to worry about. I felt no premonitions of any sort.

SEVEN

On Thursday of Holy Week, the church remembers the Last Supper. The readings tell of the breaking of bread and sharing of the cup of wine, of Jesus' acting as a servant to His disciples by washing their feet, of His foretelling of His betrayal and of Peter's denial. The service is a solemn one, with only a few hymns. At the end, the altar is stripped, and all the things that remind one of Christ are removed from the sanctuary.

Gone are all the crosses, all the remains of the communion gifts, and all the candles. The Gospel Book is removed, as is the Lectern Bible. Even such little things as the book markers and the cloth on the credence table. Then the members of the altar party file quietly out of the sanctuary as the lights are dimmed.

We pray in the darkened church, and when we are ready to leave, we do so without talking to our neighbours. We go home to reflect on the events of that Thursday night so long ago: of Jesus praying in the garden, of His disciples' failure to understand what was happening, of His betrayal, and His arrest. These next two days are the darkest hours in the ecclesiastical year.

On Friday morning the Good Friday service is held. It is a legal holiday, yet few people come to church, something I would not understand until after the service. Come to think of it, I'd never gone to church on Good Friday until this year. Now, I'll never miss it as long as I can walk, creep or crawl, or be wheeled into church.

The Good Friday service is a continuation of the Maundy Thursday liturgy, as if you had never left the church. As the Thursday service ended in silence, so this one starts, with the church still stripped of all the symbols of our faith. As we kneel in prayer in the quiet church, the Officiant and his assistants silently enter, bowing solemnly before the altar. After a further period of silent prayer come the readings, hymns and the psalm, the sermon, the Solemn Intercession and the Veneration of the Cross.

Then comes the Meditation on the Cross of Jesus, a portion of the liturgy that strikes me to the heart and leaves me reeling as from a blow. In it we have read to us a mournful litany of our iniquities, making us cry out to God for our redemption. Line after line of our collective sins against our God, against our Christ and against our neighbours, the population of this earth, are read to us. We plead over and over in response, "Holy God, holy and mighty, holy and immortal one, have mercy on us." We are left here, crying for mercy, as the priest and the choir slowly file out of the sanctuary, and we quietly get up and leave.

No wonder so few people come. Most are seeking a comfortable God, not one who assails them with a blow by blow account of their transgressions. This day we are being reminded that God grieves that we have forsaken Him. To me, it has become the most significant service of the year, the day I am reminded that I still have a long way to go in the faith, the day I have to take our sins against Christ onto my shoulders and bear the burden. It is a burden that each of us must carry alone. It will be at the great Easter Vigil on Saturday night before we are relieved of this burden, as we again leave the church in silent meditation.

EIGHT

It was hard to get my mind back on my work. I arrived at the airport about noon and checked the schedule. The Merediths had departed for Georgetown and Terry was preparing for his trip to Las Vegas. Ralph's gleaming Twin Comanche sat on the ramp in front of the flight school and Terry supervised while Ralph filed an instrument flight plan. That afternoon, I had scheduled an evaluation checkride for each of our two new commercial students. I was looking forward to flying with Zane Rossiter, dreading my session with Lance Brock.

Zane was scheduled first and was waiting for me half an hour before his scheduled flight. He had obtained a pre-flight checklist from Gayla and was reading through it, cross-referencing it with his Cessna 150 manual. I was pleased to see this sign of serious contemplation of the task ahead.

We went out to the flight line and I watched Zane do the pre-flight.

"I want you to tell me each thing that you are doing, how you are doing it, and why."

"Okay," he agreed happily. Following the checklist, he went over every inch of the small, two-seat trainer, showing and explaining as he went. Another mark in the plus column. He hesitated a bit with the radio communications, not comfortable using the school's abbreviation instead of the full call sign.

"Since we aren't going on a cross-country this time, use the school call sign," I explained. "So today, use 'Robin 3.' Any time you leave this tower's area, you use the full registration mark. The school call signs are a special agreement with this particular tower. We did that because several of our planes have registrations that are similar to each other or to other planes based here at Exeter. It avoids confusion."

"Roger," he replied, slipping easily into aviation jargon.

Zane used the printed checklist to do a thorough run-up, switched from ground control to the tower frequency, and requested take-off clearance. He had shown the foresight of asking me in advance where our practice area was located, and had looked it up on his chart. Now he turned to a heading that would take us to that area.

This guy is too good to be true, I thought. The nasty little demon that infects flight instructor's minds crept into mine. I would have to create some emergency or distraction to see if all this polished proficiency would crumble like a clod of dirt when something unexpected happened. Before I could think of some sneaky trick to play on him, he said, "If my engine quit now, I'd try to put it right there." He pointed to an open tract of land beside the highway, just off the departure end of the runway.

Even in the sneaky trick department, I couldn't keep up with him!

With my mind drifting off to the morning church service, I found that I was the one who was half a step behind everything that the student did. It should have been the other way around. When I gave him a simulated engine failure, he responded with professional calm. He immediately trimmed the plane at an airspeed that would give him maximum range in his glide. While doing this, his neck was swivelling to find the best spot for an emergency landing. Once he had selected a suitable place to land, he set up an approach to it, and began to imitate the trouble shooting that he would need to do in a real emergency. He pulled on carburetor heat, checked the fuel selector valve, the mixture control and the primer. All were in the proper position. He reported that the fuel tanks were nearly full, and since he had checked them in his pre-flight, he knew that it wasn't a matter of inoperative gauges. Of course he knew what the real trouble was. I had closed the throttle and was holding onto it firmly so that he couldn't use it.

Zane made a pretty decent approach to his chosen field. I'd have taken a different one, but then I knew the terrain. He would have made a survivable landing, but before we actually turned our make-believe emergency into a real one, I gave him back the power and we climbed on out again.

Was there any way I could rattle this guy? Flight instructors tend to be wary of the smooth-as-silk pilots who do things too perfectly. I distracted his attention, simulated a variety of emergencies, gave him spins. Nothing fazed him. It was not until we entered the circuit on our way back to the airport that I discovered what could confuse and distract him. It wasn't anything that I did. It wasn't anything that Dale had taught, or failed to teach him. It was the work of some anonymous check pilot at some big flight school in Vancouver where they tried to make airline pilots out of the greenest of novices.

Zane made a nice entry into the circuit, flying parallel to the runway on the downwind at exactly the correct altitude. It was when we started our descent to land that things fell apart like a kid dropping a bag of marbles.

Abeam the runway threshold, he reduced power, staring at the airspeed indicator and the tachometer as he did so. He had to juggle the throttle around a bit to get exactly the right power setting. By the time he had adjusted the power to his satisfaction, the plane had nosed down into a steeper descent than he wanted and he was drifting in toward the runway. He noticed the increase in airspeed, frowned and hesitated. While trying to figure out what was going on, his ingrained training, ala Dale, caused him to unconsciously pull back on the elevator control, but while he was doing this, he reluctantly decreased his carefully set power.

By this time he had extended his downwind out quite a ways beyond the runway threshold. Looking back over his shoulder at the runway, he realized that he was lower than he should have been. Instead of increasing his power, he pulled the nose up. We hit a spot of turbulence and the stall warning horn, which tells you when you are getting too slow for comfort, gave a little bleep. Zane

64

automatically, and correctly, pushed the nose back down, increasing the airspeed. By now, we were way out and very low. The old training finally kicked in and he advanced the throttle until the added power stopped our descent.

"Oh, oh! I need flaps." He shoved the flap lever down and watched the indicator, which was placed low down on the instrument panel, so that he lost his outside visual reference. He stopped the flaps at 10°. We were already a mile off the end of the runway and as I expected, a call from the tower crackled over the airwaves with the polite message, "Robin 3, you are clear to turn base any time. There's a Dash 8 on downwind behind you. When you land, minimum time on the runway please."

This was the first distraction that seemed to fluster him. He hauled the 150 over into a steep bank with poorly coordinated use of the controls. As soon as he rolled out, I could hear him muttering, "Flaps 20°." He stared at the indicator while the flaps went down. By this time, we had overshot final approach and he had to make more than a 90° turn to get back on course. The increased power had now produced a climb of a couple hundred feet, so down went the nose, which increased the airspeed, so back came the power. That stopped our climb, which was what we needed in the first place. Our entire approach consisted of a series of these inappropriate changes in power and pitch, interrupted by periods of time for carefully putting down further exact increments of flaps until they were entirely extended to 40°. We arrived somewhere near the runway threshold, and Zane's confidence returned. He made a pretty decent landing.

After we had exited the runway and tuned in ground control, I told Zane to request clearance back for another takeoff. When we had received the clearance and were headed back toward the departure end of the runway, I squirmed around in my seat to face him.

"That was absolutely the worst approach I've had the misfortune to ride through in the last ten years! What the hell were you doing?"

"I guess I'm a little out of practice."

"*What* have you been practicing?"

"I could land the Super Cub okay. I've always had trouble with the newer planes unless I keep at it all the time and really concentrate."

"The Super Cub is a small, two-place, high-wing airplane. The 150 is a small, two-place, high-wing airplane."

"Well, the Cub is an older style taildragger."

"Super Cubs were being made after Cessna 150s had gone out of production. Furthermore, nose wheels are to hold up the engine while taxiing. Tail wheels are to keep the tail from literally dragging. Neither one of them has any function in a landing approach. You didn't get any of this crap from Dale, I know."

Zane came to a stop in the run-up area and turned sheepishly to face me.

"You're right. I started having trouble when I got checked out in Vancouver. Some young dude in a uniform that looks like ones the airline pilots wear gave me this procedure to follow. It's like you've got to do it this way because the professionals do."

"Professionals fly whatever airplane they are flying in the proper way for that airplane," I interjected.

"Well this dude said I had to follow this procedure to the letter. He said it was the way they do it in jets so I should learn it that way to begin with."

"A Cessna 150 is *not* a jet!" I fumed.

"He sort of made me feel like a hick from the sticks since I'd learned up in Whitehorse in an old type of plane. He said I needed to start using a professional procedure." I could tell that this assessment had really hurt his ego.

"Just what was the procedure?"

"First you've got to reduce your power to 1500 RPM to slow down to 80. Then you've got to put down 10° of flaps. Then you turn base. Then you put down another 10° of flaps and reduce your power to slow to 70. Then you turn final and put down another 10° of flaps. Then you slow to 65. Then you put down the last of the flaps. Then you slow to 60."

"What do you do for altitude control?"

"You lower the nose if you're too high and raise it if you're too low."

"And you had trouble getting the hang of it?"

"Yeah," he admitted, avoiding my angry eyes. "I have a hard time getting it all together."

"No wonder. Because it's a bunch of rot."

Zane stared at me, open-mouthed.

"Can you remember what Dale taught you?"

Zane frowned, thinking.

I asked, "Did you ever get too low on final and have Dale verbally rap you on the knuckles for it?"

Zane grinned and nodded.

"What did Dale tell you?"

"'Don't try to stretch the glide,'" Zane answered with alacrity.

"What does that mean to you?"

"Uh — I'm not sure what you're getting at."

"Let's go back out to the practice area and I'll show you. And I'm going to add one thing to what I expect of you." As Zane looked at me questioningly, I added, my voice dripping sarcasm, "You committed one of the most unpardonable sins in all of aviation while you were making that approach."

"What was that?" he asked tentatively, not really wanting the answer.

"All nine of the Snowbirds could have flown right past your nose in formation and you wouldn't have noticed them!"

Zane blushed at the insult, but nodded in assent.

"From now on I want you to point out to me everything moving in the sky, whether it's a bird or a jet at 35,000 feet."

We climbed back out and headed for the practice area. I had Zane level off at a precise altitude and simulate a circuit to a runway 1000 feet lower.

"Now, we're going to see what individual controls on this airplane do. First, we're going to try out the throttle. Take your left hand off the yoke and hold it in the air. Keep your right hand on the throttle. Reduce the power about 500 RPMs. Don't bother about being exact." Zane did what I had told him. "Now look at the airspeed indicator—*after* checking for traffic. What has happened to your airspeed?"

"It's increased," Zane exclaimed in amazement.

"Why is that?"

"I suppose because the nose dropped down."

"What happened to your altitude?"

"We lost some."

"Now, I've got the throttle and you have the yoke. Without changing power, I want you to raise the nose. Look for traffic first."

Zane took a long look out the windows on all sides, and smugly reported a jet flying overhead. We had started this manoeuvre at a slow airspeed, as would be used in a landing approach. "What's happening to our airspeed?"

"We've slowed down."

"Right. Now to get back to Dale saying, 'Don't try to stretch your glide.' What was he talking about?"

"That if you got low on final, don't try to make it to the runway by pulling up the nose."

"Exactly. What you were doing on the approach you made was to try to control speed with the throttle and altitude with the elevator control. It doesn't work, though you can get the impression that it does. What happens is that when you reduce power, you lose altitude, so you pull the nose up thinking it will keep you from going down, but what it does is increase the angle of attack and slow your airspeed. What is meant by 'angle of attack'?"

"The angle at which the wing meets the airflow."

"That's close enough. When your angle of attack increases, your airspeed slows but your lift increases, slowing your descent.

You get the impression that you slowed the plane by reducing power. You didn't. You slowed the plane by increasing your angle of attack. You started your descent by reducing power. You accomplished in four steps what you could have done in one if you had the proper idea of which control does what. Pretend you're in the Super Cub. Fly the approach like Dale taught you."

"Half the flaps on downwind and the rest when you need them on final?"

"Okay. And keep the approach in close. We're not going on a cross-country. Head up. Look for traffic. To help you concentrate on essentials, I'm going to cover up the airspeed indicator and the tachometer."

"Oh, yeah. I remember *that!*"

"You should be able to tell your approximate power setting by the sound of the engine, and your airspeed by the position of the nose in relation to the horizon. Don't bother looking at the instrument panel. There's nothing to see there."

Zane slid back into his old habits with the greatest of ease and made two very good landings. Now I had him pegged. The kind of thing that could throw him off was something that offended his logical mind. Trying to make reason out of chaos could occupy his mind almost completely, to the detriment of everything else. What he needed most in his training was the confidence to challenge anyone who tried to force him into doing something that did not make sense to him. But the danger in that was in whether he could distinguish between the illogical and the merely unfamiliar. I'd need to get to know him a lot better.

As we taxied in, we called on the school's radio frequency and ordered fuel. I would use the same plane when I flew with Lance. Lance was waiting at the desk. He watched Zane as we walked in, an air of nervousness about him. He clasped and unclasped a hand that hung at his side, breathed in shallow respirations as if taking a deep breath might make him explode, and followed Zane with eyes that showed an agony of envy. I was astonished at the change from his usual surly defensiveness.

After a brief talk with Zane, in the privacy of my office, I went to Lance and jerking my head toward the flight line, said, "Let's go." He almost jumped out the door and strode eagerly toward the plane. I followed the same procedure with him as with Zane. I found out later that Gayla had warned him that I was a stickler for using printed checklists and had dug up copies for him. He needed more prompting than Zane, and more things had to be explained to him. Usually when I was halfway through an explanation, I'd see the memory flood back into his face. In the back of his mind, he knew all this stuff. It just needed to be dragged out and dusted off.

"What if you saw a few wave-like ripples when you looked down the metal on this surface?" I asked. That one seemed to stump him. I went on, "Later in the course, you'll fly the Bonanza. Let's go look at it."

As we stopped beside the sleek six-seat retractable, I saw the look of longing on Lance's homely face. I ran my hand down a thin strip of aluminium running along the thickest part of the wing. "This is called the spar cap. Why is it called that?"

"I guess it is over the wing spar." He was practically drooling at the sight of the Bonanza.

"That's right. Now suppose you sighted down the spar cap, like this." I suited action to word. "Suppose I saw that instead of being absolutely smooth, there were some wrinkles in it. Would that cause me any concern?"

"I guess so."

"It would make my stomach turn a flip-flop, that's what it would do! Why?"

"I guess it would mean that something had happened to the spar."

"Right on! And what do you think might happen if you flew it that way?"

He grinned and said flippantly, "The wing might fall off."

"You're absolutely right. You would be seeing evidence that the wing spar has been damaged and might not hold up in flight. Now let's go back over to the 150."

Lance looked back wistfully over his shoulder as we left the Bonanza. You're going to have to be a very good boy, kiddo, before I let you fly that one, I thought. The A36 Bonanza had cost me way up in six figures even second hand and I had only a few payments left before it really became mine. It was finally paying its way with the income it generated. I had nightmares about something happening to it just as I was finishing three years of stress-ridden worry over the payments.

I turned my attention back to the task at hand. "Now let's extrapolate to the 150. What would ripples in the skin signify to you?"

"That there might be damage to structural members underneath." I almost yelled Hooray. Then Lance brought me down to earth again.

"You don't really need to do this thorough a pre-flight every time though, do you? I mean, it wastes a lot of time."

"If it saves your life, do you consider the time wasted?"

"But…"

"Every time you go flying, you need to do a thorough pre-flight."

"But you just flew this plane and it was all right."

"How do you know that we didn't spin out of a departure stall and get into a secondary stall after recovering from the spin, putting all kinds of stress on the airframe?"

"But you'd have said something."

I threw my hands up in the air. "*If* we realized it and *if* we bothered to tell you."

His long, thin face creased into a frown. I watched him as he thought it over. He had a long nose, narrowly spaced eyes, and his thin-lipped mouth was too wide for his face. His mousy brown hair, cut in the current style that gave the impression that someone had put a bowl over his head and used a electric shaver on anything that stuck out, came to a point in front and defied all efforts to comb it down smooth. He was of average height, and that put him about an inch shorter than my stature: I'm very tall for a woman. Whenever he was around me, he tried to pull himself up out of his natural slouch and stretch his height to its limit. Remembering his envious looks in Zane's direction and adding to it my perception that his vanity was affronted by the presence of a taller woman, I thought I'd do a little name-dropping.

"Do you follow the space shots at all?"

"Oh sure. I always watch them."

"I remember an astronaut being interviewed on TV. They asked him if he ever had a sick feeling as the rocket was lifting off that maybe he had forgotten something, and he said, 'No. The checklists are too thorough'."

Lance watched me through narrowed eyes.

"There's another story I like. A bunch of pilots were hanging around an airport watching another pilot pre-flight an airplane, using a printed checklist. They were laughing among themselves and saying, 'Hey, look at the novice.' Then someone else there asked if they knew who the 'novice' pilot was. They didn't. 'That's Charles Lindbergh'."

Lance's gaze dropped. He's only halfway convinced, I thought. Well, that's better than nothing.

All through the rest of the session, Lance struggled hard to remember what he had been taught as a student here. He was really trying. He had considerable natural ability and once he remembered the correct way to perform a manoeuvre, he did it with ease. His problem as a pilot was one of attitude. He could have been a very proficient pilot if he had wanted to be. Now he was trying, and I felt a thrill of pleasure in the anticipation that he might change his ways and start taking all aspects of flying seriously.

After he had gone home, I said something to that effect to Gayla, who commented, "He wants to be like Zane."

"D'you think so?"

"He knew you were flying with this good-looking guy and he watched when you came back and saw those greased-on landings Zane made. He said, 'I can fly like that.' I said I hoped he could, 'cause he'd have to if he wanted to get along with you. He got this real determined look on his face and said, 'I'll show 'em that I can fly just as good.' So I said, 'Good for you.' So he said, 'You mean that?' I said, 'Sure!' I hope he does."

"I hope so, too. He has a lot of natural ability, but he needs to use it right. He needs a lot of polish."

Well, well! So a little jealousy was behind all this! I was glad that Lance hadn't been looking when Zane had made his first disastrous approach. The jealousy might have turned into arrogance. I resolved to schedule Lance just after Zane on a regular basis. I recalled the expression on Lance's face when I had come in with Zane. Lance could never compete in the looks category. He could have taken the path of contemptuous rebellion. Instead he had picked up the gauntlet, accepted the challenge and decided to work. Good for him!

NINE

Both the young men flew with me again on Saturday, as I assessed their proficiency in cross-country flying. Lance was not scheduled until two hours after Zane, but when I returned from lunch, I found them both in the pilot lounge, heads down over a chart, surrounded by the impedimenta of navigational planning: flight logs, plotters, flight computers, coloured highlighting pens and reference manuals. Zane seemed to be explaining something to Lance, who showed keen interest. I had told Zane to plan a flight to Calgary. We wouldn't go all the way, only get well established on our course. I would then give him a diversion to an alternate followed by some instrument flying, where he would put on a visor that allowed him to see the instrument panel, but not anything outside the plane. We took Robin 4, a Cessna 172, which had more navigation equipment than the 150s, but did not have the GPS that Robin 5 contained. That was a luxury students could learn about later.

I had told Lance to plan a flight to Victoria, over on Vancouver Island, and as I walked out the door with Zane, I saw Lance get down to work, leaning over the chart, elbows on the table, his spindly gams wrapped around a chair leg, baseball cap pushed to the back of his head.

Zane did his usual proficient job, his confidence having been restored. When we walked back into the office Lance was waiting and watching in envy as Zane, whistling cheerfully, twirled the instrument hood around his index finger. I spent some time going over Lance's flight plan. He had done a creditable job.

As I flew with Lance, I discovered something about him that I had not been aware of, though a niggling memory of some remark Ace Flynn had made hung in the back of my mind. Lance had an extraordinary sense of where he was. "There's Fiske Lake.

Boy did I catch some big rainbows there last summer." Or, "The road to Salt Creek should be on the other side of this ridge."

Zane had stayed precisely on course by minute attention to detail, even though the terrain was unfamiliar. Lance occasionally strayed off his course, but his incredible knowledge of the local terrain always bailed him out. Different people; different gifts!

Jan would now be taking over Zane's training. I went over the results of Zane's evaluation flights with her, telling her where I thought he needed more work. I signed him off in our school files to fly solo. I would keep flying with Lance until Terry returned. Lance could only fly one more day before he went back to work on Monday so he scheduled two flights the following afternoon. The fact that Zane was allowed to fly solo and he was not rankled and he showed signs of rebellion.

"You can fly solo later this afternoon if you show me some good progress on this flight," I told him. He buckled down and worked hard, and I let him go solo, giving him a list of the things I wanted him to work on. The resentment melted.

I wished that it were Lance who could fly every day and Zane who could only fly on weekends. If Lance could have kept up with Zane, I felt that the competition would do him good. I crossed my fingers and hoped.

Early Saturday evening as I relaxed at home with Cloud Nine on my lap, I received two phone calls. The first was from Penny.

"I went out with Zane last night." She sounded coy.

"How'd it go?"

"Great! He's sure an interesting person."

"I thought you'd had it with men." She and I had both expressed this sentiment on numerous occasions.

"Well... *some* men."

"Penny, be careful."

"Yes, Mummy."

I was glad my blush couldn't travel over the phone line. "I didn't mean it that way."

"I know. But he is a lot of fun. It was an old-fashioned sort of date. He called for me at my place, helped me on with my coat, helped me into the car and all that. He's a perfect gentleman. Guess what he arrived in, by the way."

"A Mercedes," I teased.

"No. Guess again."

"A golden coach with matching Palomino horses."

"Be serious!"

"I don't have to guess. He drives up every day in an Astro van. Don't tell me he called for you in that."

Penny chuckled. "As a matter of fact, he didn't. He called for me in a rented limousine. He said the van wasn't very clean."

I was impressed and said so.

"We went to Charles'."

"Big time! I hope he paid the bill."

"Oh, Robin!" Penny exclaimed in exasperation. "Of *course* he did."

"When he took you home, how did he act?"

"Now, Mummy! I told you he was a gentleman. He kissed my hand, would you believe. Sort of as a joke, actually, because I told him no kisses on the first date. That's a polite way of saying no nothing else either."

"You didn't invite him in, I take it."

"No, Mummy. And he didn't invite me to his place."

She was happy in a bubbly sort of way and I was happy for her. We gabbled on for a while as Penny released some of that effervescence. It was catching: I found myself joining in her celebration. After she had hung up, Betty Forsythe called.

"Guess what Douglas did today."

"I haven't the faintest. What?"

"He got a dog."

"Sneaky, isn't he? I assume that he didn't ask your advice first."

"He did *not!*"

"What kind of a dog?"

"It seems to be a cross between a German Shepherd and some kind of hunting dog. He says he just happened to be in the area of the animal shelter (likely story) and decided to drop by. He looked at all the dogs and this great galumphing creature took to him. It jumped up on him, licked his face and cried when he started to leave, so he forked over 35 bucks and brought the beast home. Well, I took one look at it and said he'd better take it to the vet and have it checked over, so we called that lady vet who's a friend of yours…"

"Chris Whitney?"

"Yes. So Douglas took the dog over there, and I guess Dr. Whitney looked him over (the dog that is) with a jaundiced eye and said he had fleas and ringworm. Well, Douglas decided he'd give the dog back to the shelter. They let you take the dog to a vet for a free exam and if the vet finds a problem, the shelter will accept it back. But Dr. Whitney said he'd better bring home some flea stuff. Premise spray, she called it. We spent the rest of the afternoon de-fleaing the house and vacuuming up every last hair in case the dog had shed any ringworm spores. I'm exhausted!"

"So, are you going to get even by sneaking out and getting some great hulking tomcat?"

"I'm thinking about it. Believe me, I'm thinking about it!"

The Great Vigil of Easter began outside the door of the church just after dark. A small fire of wood shavings was kindled and from this the Pascal candle was lit. This large candle, with symbols pressed into the wax, was then carried by our cantor, Kevin Dann, a tenor who Betty had persuaded to join the choir on the first Sunday she was here. He had a clear, high voice, well suited to liturgical chants.

As he carried the candle up the steps, parishioners flanking his path lit small candles from the large one and followed him into the church. At the top of the steps, the cantor paused, raised the candle high over his head and chanted, "The light of Christ." The people responded, "Thanks be to God."

He entered the darkened church and pausing as he turned to walk down the nave, held the candle on high. "The light of Christ."

"Thanks be to God," we chanted.

The cantor continued toward the altar, stopping before it, and held the candle aloft again. "The light of Christ."

"Thanks be to God."

The cantor then rendered another chant, performed by a deacon if one is present. I learned from my program that it is called the Exsultet. We were gathered around the Easter candle, it and the small candles we carried providing the only light in the church.

> *"Rejoice heavenly powers! Sing choirs of angels!*
> *Exult, all creation around God's throne!*
> *Jesus Christ, our King, is risen!*
> *Sound the trumpet of salvation!..."*

After this long chant of praise, the church lights were switched on, we put out our candles and found our seats while the Pascal candle was placed in its stand. It would be used at baptisms and other special ceremonies until the following Easter. It would also burn at all services in the church until the day of Pentecost.

There were many readings at this service. The one assigned to me, my first-ever reading in the church, was the story of the Israelites' deliverance out of Egypt; the familiar story of the parting of the Red Sea. I had come early to mark the place in the Lectern Bible and had found Owen Dunphy there, industriously marking the pages of all the readings.

"Which is yours?" he asked.

"Exodus 14:10 to 15:1."

Owen made a great display of finding the place and gave me a lecture on the use of the mike, the necessity of projecting my voice and the importance of pronouncing names correctly. I knew all that and had trouble hiding my impatience. I am *not* going to tell him off in church, I reminded myself. Wait until I get him in a dark alley somewhere! I had practiced aloud, over and over until it was nearly memorized. I had identified the trouble spots and was sure I could get through without error. Would Owen kindly go away and leave me alone!

Owen was the first reader. He was good. He could put animation into the account in Genesis of creation. He believed it literally. I thought of it as a story told to illustrate to people who had no written word, that the earth was God's creation. Such stories had to be memorable so they could be handed down from generation to generation through the oral tradition. It was only when I realized that I did not have to believe that this was literally, word for word, written by God that I was able to accept the Christian faith.

Owen did tend to sound pompous, but on the whole, he was one of the better readers in our church.

When my turn came, I stepped up to the lectern and adjusted the mike. The second reader had been Eleanor Ware who was a foot shorter than I, and even standing on a stool, could barely be seen by the congregation. I read in my best speaking voice. The words flowed freely from my mouth. This is a scene of great action, of the sea parting and the Israelites looking back at the pursuing Egyptian army, of chariot wheel clogging and horses and charioteers being thrown into the sea as the water rushes back behind the retreating Israelites. I tried to dramatize it, to make it sound exciting and climactic. I was told after the service, by several parishioners, that I had read very well. Even Douglas congratulated me. I couldn't have been more thrilled.

This service marks the beginning of the celebration of Christ's resurrection. The liturgical colour has changed to white, the colour of purity, the colour worn at the great celebrations of the church. The "Alleluias," absent during Lent and Holy Week, had returned. The atmosphere was one of joy, of release, of awe at the miracle of the resurrection.

Yet not many people attended this service. I wondered if they knew what they were missing.

TEN

On Easter Sunday, everyone comes to church. All the closet Anglicans, known as the "C and Es", who only come on Christmas Eve and Easter, were present. Extra chairs had been set up in the back, and people squeezed together to make room. There was more than the usual amount of music, with a trumpeter, a choir anthem, and Lynne McDowell, our leading soprano singing a solo. Otherwise I don't remember much about the service. It was like most of the others, perhaps more joyful.

As we left after the service, I wormed my way through the crowd to catch up with Penny and Paul. When I got near them, I heard another voice, Owen's, expounding on some subject or other. I stopped in my tracks and let the exodus flow around me. I drifted along with the current, keeping several people between myself and Owen. I'd leave my friends to extricate themselves, I thought. Owen could be hard to ditch once he'd gotten started on one of his pet topics.

Finally, Penny and Paul turned up in the church hall for coffee, looking slightly frazzled.

"What was Owen spouting off about?" I asked.

"He's on to some kind of financial shenanigans and has gone home to work on the problem. He's tickled pink," Paul explained.

"His shenanigans or someone else's?"

"Someone else's, of course. He'd never be caught doing something fishy."

Penny took up the narrative. "He said he'd been suspicious of something he found in one of the accounts he handled. This was about a month ago. He wasn't sure, but when the same thing came up a week ago and he found another incident yesterday, he realized he was onto something criminal. He was going to go home and work on it so he could get it all figured out before he left on his trip. I guess he's put the trip off until he's finished with this problem."

"You know how Owen can be." Paul mimicked Owen's voice. "'On the first day, I gather all the data. On the second day, I collate it. On the third day, I go to the bank and tell them to look up their depositor's name and give it to the police, and I get in touch with Revenue Canada.' You know how he likes to be biblical."

"Maybe he'll forget about Compline," I suggested hopefully.

"I doubt it. Owen never lets his work interfere with his desire to set the rest of us on the right path." We all laughed.

"Penny and I are going to the Lakeview Terrace instead. Too bad you're not going to be here to go with us."

"I'll make it up some other time. Now I'd better get home and pick up my bag. I'm all ready to leave. My flight to Vancouver goes out at 2:20, and from there I leave for London at seven o'clock."

"Have a good trip. I wish I were going with you."

"I've got to take Paul to the airport," Penny told me. "We'd better go. I'll see you at six o'clock, Robin. I made a reservation."

As Paul and Penny left, I drifted over to a group where Faith was conversing with some other ladies. She was much more outgoing and socially inclined since Clive had come along. As I was thinking about this, Clive himself appeared at the door, glanced around, and spotting Faith, came over to join the group. Douglas casually dropped by as well.

"I'd better go," Faith told the other ladies. "I'm sure Clive will want to get back to his hockey game."

"It doesn't start for a while, love. Don't leave on my account." Clive's voice was bluff and hearty, just a little too loud.

"Have you all met Clive?" Faith asked, and seeing that several of the others had not, she introduced him around the group. The ladies shouldered their way closer, most seeming to go gaga over this expensively attired hunk. "And here is our dear

Rector," she concluded, taking Douglas by the hand. "But you have already met him."

"Yes, yes. I have," Clive boomed. "Faith is fortunate to have such excellent spiritual guidance. From you, sir, as well as from your other minister, Reverend Marriott. Such a wonderful lady."

Whenever someone professes something so vehemently, I wonder if they are not trying to convince themselves as much as to make a statement to other people. As usual, Clive had my hackles up. However, the conversation drifted onto the subject of sports.

"Hockey is all right, but it's not really my game," Clive stated. "Now, Australian Rules Football, that's another story. I can get quite passionate about that."

"Did you ever play the game?" Douglas asked.

"Only as a student, back in Australia. But I've always remained a fan. Whenever I get a chance to watch it on TV, I do. I'm a Hawks fan, of course."

"Hawks?"

"Hawthorn Hawks. Because of my name, you know."

"That sounds practical. You won't ever forget who you're supposed to be rooting for."

"And a good team to cheer for, too. They're consistently one of the best."

"Do you have a favourite hockey team?" I asked.

"Oh, the Canucks, of course."

"When did you come to Canada from Australia?" one of the ladies asked. "I have a cousin in Australia. Do you know…"

"Oh, I've been in Canada for many years. My dear wife, who just passed away…" here his voice dropped to a lower register, "…and I emigrated right after we were married. We were attracted by the oil fields. Seemed like a good place to get a start in life."

"Not much of a place for a woman, though. What was your wife's name?" The question came from Gretchen Schmidt, our resident feminist. She had previously remained aloof. No mere man ever made an impression on her.

"I beg your pardon?" Clive said leaning toward the speaker.

"Your wife's name?"

"Oh. Alice. Her name was Alice."

"What did Alice think of life on the Canadian frontier?"

Clive laughed. "She was a good sport. It was rough at first, but she adapted." Unimpressed, Gretchen frowned her disapproval.

Clive turned toward me, put on his best salesman voice, so that I knew he was about to make a pitch for some project or other, and set forth a proposition. "Robin, I've been thinking. I'd like to invite you to a Toastmasters' event one of these days. You should join. There's a ladies group. They'd love to hear you talk about flying."

"No thanks," I replied in an offhanded way, trying to indicate my complete indifference to the suggestion.

"You'd enjoy it."

"I doubt it," I stated bluntly.

"We have a lot of fun." He paused and I tried to hide behind the activity of finishing off my coffee and placing the empty cup on a tray being passed around by one of the ladies of the parish. "We get together to have a meal and exchange stories."

"We do that here in church."

"Oh, you do? You have fun evenings, I suppose. Potluck dinners?"

"That's not what I mean. At every church service, we share a meal with Jesus Christ, and tell the story of our faith."

"Oh." He sounded deflated. I chanced a quick glance at his lugubrious facade. Before he could get back on his previous track, I commanded, "Now when you marry Faith, don't prevent her from attending church."

"I wouldn't think of it! Anything Faith wants, she'll have."

Clive pushed up his cuff and ostentatiously consulted his Rolex. Why anyone needs a watch that costs in the five figures, merely to tell the time, is beyond me. But of course, the least of the functions of such a timepiece is actually to disclose the hour of the day. "Well, I guess we'd better get on our way. The game starts at two."

Faith and Clive made their departure, amid many cheerful farewells from the group, who then fell into fervent and proficient gossiping. I drifted away. Douglas had already found another group, and as the crowd thinned out, he deftly snared Betty and they made their escape.

I stopped at Penny's apartment at six. We usually went places in my pickup truck rather than in her tiny car. The front passenger seat of the car was always piled with teaching materials from her job, bags of things she had bought but hadn't yet unloaded, magazines and sweaters or coats in case the weather changed. To ride in her car one had to shovel enough of this material into the back seat to create room to sit down. Though I generally have the odd propeller blade or wheel faring in the back of my pickup, I try to keep the passenger seat empty enough to accommodate what it was meant for, people.

As I often do at buffets, I loaded my plate with so many salads, I hardly had room on the plate or in my stomach for the roast beef, the fish casserole and the potatoes and vegetables. But the dessert table beckoned, and groaning, I dutifully picked out a couple of pastries. We ate in relaxed companionship. Penny is one person I don't have to put on a front to impress. We can both merely be ourselves.

As we left the dining room, which overlooked the lake, sparkling with the reflections of waterfront lights, we ran into Zane Rossiter. He put on an act of surprise at finding us there, but I suspected that he'd been waiting. On finding that I had my own vehicle to get home in, he asked Penny to join him in the bar.

"Go ahead, Penny. I've enjoyed our evening together, but I'm going home and hit the hay anyway. Go have fun."

Later Penny told me they had gone to a movie and Zane had taken her home about one AM. Ah, youth! If I tried to do that, I'd be a wreck the next day.

On Monday morning, the Merediths returned from Georgetown, full of exuberance and tales of spectacular snow-covered scenery sparkling under a brilliant sun. Lance had to go back to work and couldn't fly until Saturday. Zane called to say he was making a trip to Vancouver. He had found a condo that he liked, had decided to buy it and move his base of operations to Exeter. The condo was vacant, so he could move in immediately, and he was going to pack up his computer equipment, load it in his Astro van and move it to his newfound home. He would be gone two days.

I was itching to go flying, and considered pulling my deHaviland Chipmunk military trainer out of the hangar, going out and turning it upside down. I hadn't done any aerobatics since last summer, and felt the urge to get my proficiency back to a comfortable level.

The phone rang. Joyce answered it and signalled that the call was for me. I was surprised to hear Clive's voice.

"Faith and I wondered whether you'd fly us to Vancouver."

"We'd be glad to. When do you want to go?"

"Today. We're going to honeymoon in Australia and Faith needs to get all her papers in order. We've got an appointment at the Australian Consulate first thing tomorrow morning and we wanted to go down today so we can be there bright and early. We have friends to stay with."

"Do you want us to just drop you off, or stay over and bring you back tomorrow?"

"Stay over. We should be done by noon."

"In that case, there will be a charge for the pilot's motel and meals and for waiting time."

"Oh, sure. I know that. That's quite all right. We weren't sure you could get away on short notice. I'm glad you can."

I didn't usually fly charters myself. I said, "My usual charter pilot is away on another flight, but I have another one here who I can free up. I'll make sure she can go on an overnight."

"Oh, but we want *you* to fly us down. Here, you'd better talk to Faith."

Faith's cultured tones came over the line. "When Clive suggested that we get you to fly us down, I was very hesitant. But then I thought of your experience and I felt it would be quite safe to fly with you. I'm a wee bit nervous…" she laughed her fluttery little laugh, "…but I think it might be quite an adventure. My first husband was a pilot, you know. He was taking flight training with the RCAF. He was killed in a crash. Not a plane crash, a car crash. We'd been married less than two weeks."

"How terrible! I didn't know."

"It's something I never talked about."

That was an understatement. She never talked about anything.

"Clive has been so good for me. I'm beginning to be able to talk about my past and put it all behind me."

In the background, I could hear Clive murmur a soothing phrase.

I quoted my rates, told them approximately how much the overnight stay would be, and asked when they wanted to get there. Faith sounded dismayed at the motel rates I quoted, having visions of flea-traps, but I assured her that I knew a nice motel and that I had no desire to stay at the Hilton, which she had suggested. I told her that I usually flew people into Vancouver East Airport rather than Vancouver International.

"If you go into International, you have to go over to the hangar side of the airport and there's no transportation over there. You have to get a taxi and they don't like to go around there to pick people up."

Clive got back on the line. "As long as I can get a rental car at this other airport, that's okay."

"Yes, you can. Easier than at International, where the rental car places are in the terminal."

"That's fine then. When do you want us out there?"

We set a time, and I went to the hangar to tell Rod O'Donnell that I would be taking the Bonanza overnight. I felt rather excited about it; a change of pace and of scenery. I reminded myself to pack a good book in my overnight bag. Charter flights generally consist of a small amount of flying and eons of boredom. I'm quite willing to let Terry do most of it.

I had told Clive and Faith to wear warm, comfortable clothes for the flight. At 10,500 feet, where we would be cruising, the temperature would be well below freezing. The Bonanza had a good heating system, as airplanes go, but no single engine plane is really adequately heated. Faith arrived in a light green fleece sweat suit and white running shoes. Clive wore tan cords, a rust coloured corduroy jacket over a tan turtleneck, and high-topped, very expensive-looking brown shoes. He had a sense of what clothes went well together that is uncommon in men. Women spend a great deal of their time perfecting that skill.

Rod had run the Bonanza to warm up the cabin, but I offered Faith a lap robe, which she accepted. She sat directly behind me and Clive occupied the right-hand front seat. This arrangement, I explained to Clive, who wanted Faith to have the view from the front seat, was to distribute the weight better in the airplane. I remembered Eve's comments about "ballast" and used more diplomatic language in explaining this.

We climbed out of the valley in the clear spring sunshine and Faith gasped as the distant Coast Range raised its head over the western horizon. "How far away are they?" she asked.

"Over a hundred miles," I replied. "Nearer two hundred."

She gasped. "But they're so clear. Whenever I've flown on airliners, the air is always hazy."

"The air is clearer out here in the mountains. But also, we just had a storm pass through, and that drives out the haze. I expect that it'll be less hazy than normal down in the Fraser Valley as well. The forecast visibility is excellent." I was happy that Faith's first flight in a light plane could be on such a beautiful day. It wasn't rough, either. That can be a problem on fresh spring days.

I heard Faith murmur a phrase we heard often in church, "This is the day that the Lord hath made."

Amen, I thought.

As we descended into the Fraser Valley, Vancouver Centre, from whom I had been receiving traffic advisories, handed us over to Approach Control. Approach would fit us into the flow of traffic and set us up for landing at Vancouver East. This was not a requirement when flying by Visual Flight Rules, but is a luxury I like to take advantage of on charter flights. Five miles out, Approach handed us over to Vancouver East Tower, which told me that we were number four following a Queen Air on left base. I spotted the medium twin, flashed my landing light to make it easier for the pilots of the twin to identify me. Each of us acknowledged seeing the other.

As the Queen Air turned final in front of us, we were fairly close, but his approach speed would be higher, so I settled into a normal approach, knowing that there would be good separation from the twin by the time we were ready to land. My passengers, sensing my concentration on the pre-landing checks and on watching for conflicting traffic, were silent. We touched down gently and rolled off the runway at mid-field, taxiing to the tiedown area of a company I liked to do business with while in Vancouver.

The line boy directed me to a vacant spot, I went through the shut-down procedures, and finally told my passengers, "Okay. We're here! You can get out now."

"That was *wonderful!* Faith clapped her hands, and as she got up, she leaned over and gave me a kiss on the cheek. Clive helped her out of the plane, and after conversing with the line boy through the side window, I followed them. I unloaded their luggage, directed them to the office, where their rental car would be waiting, and turned my attention to securing the plane for the night. A fuel truck rumbled up. I had the tanks topped off and while the truck driver ran my company Visa card through his machine, I tied the plane down. I retrieved the journey log from the cockpit and made my entries, using the wing as a table, feeling the light breeze lift my hair and blow it into my face. The sun was warm on my back, the memory of a perfect flight fresh in my mind as I stood there beside this big, fast, powerful airplane, which I almost owned. Life was very good at that moment.

ELEVEN

"Moving up in the world, aren't you? An A36 Bonanza, no less."

I felt my body stiffen, the back of my neck tingle. I turned slowly to look up at six feet four of long, lean masculinity capped by a wind-reddened face and hair that had once been the colour of newly sawn pine lumber, but was now receding and striped with grey. My ex, Dale Carruthers.

The grey eyes that usually seemed to be up in the clouds somewhere now keenly surveyed the sleek lines of the Bonanza, while a work-roughened hand gently caressed the smooth surface of the wing. I'd always had to take a back seat to a good airplane in Dale's scheme of things; something I'd never really minded because those had been my own priorities.

"Not bad," he said with reverence.

"It's a nice plane," I replied lamely.

"Things must be going well."

"They're okay."

Dale's mind snapped back to the here and now. He turned to look at me. "Loosen up, Robin, for Christ's sake."

"I'm sorry."

"I'm admiring your bloody airplane. Is there anything wrong with that?" Childish hurt had crept into his voice.

I looked away, trying to gather up my thoughts. "You make it sound as if it was unbelievable that I could have a successful business."

"That's not what I meant," he snapped.

"Okay. Truce?"

"Truce."

"What are you doing in Vancouver? You haven't become a city dweller, have you?" I asked, making idle conversation. Dale's current living accommodations were of absolutely no interest to me.

"Not on your life! We had a Beaver down here to be rebuilt and I came down to pick it up. I test flew it today and had a couple of glitches fixed. I'm flying it back to Whitehorse tomorrow."

"Enjoying the warm weather while you're here?"

Dale grimaced. "Not really. They can have this place. It's bigger and harder to get around in every time I come down. I expect Exeter's getting pretty crowded now, too."

"It's not bad. I like it."

The conversation lagged. Dale walked around the plane, admiring it. When I'd bought the Bonanza, I'd gone through a lot of sleepless nights, especially in the winter when business was slow. It had cost a big chunk of money; way up in the six-figure range, and I had only recently begun to feel that someday it would have paid for itself. It was a good investment, I realized. Cheaper to operate than a light twin but just as fast, it was roomy and comfortable for the passengers and a dream to fly. It was also a good advertisement for the school, painted as it was in red and white, with the Red Robin logo on the tail.

His inspection of the plane completed, Dale came back around to where I was leaning against the fuselage.

"How about dinner?"

"Okay."

"Is the restaurant across the road okay with you, or do you want something fancier?" It would have been an unremarkable question if it hadn't been accompanied by a quick flick of the grey eyes toward the fancy Bonanza.

"The restaurant across the street is fine with me. I lead a simple life," I replied truculently.

Dale either didn't notice or felt it best to let the remark slide by. We walked down the entry road and across a busy street to a simple family restaurant attached to the motel where I planned to stay. Dale ordered fried chicken and I had Salisbury steak smothered in onions. We had pie, apple for Dale, lemon meringue for me, and sat drinking coffee and discussing the flying business.

Dale, ten years my senior, had taught me how to fly. I'd fallen for aviation, and for Dale. The first had become a life-long passion. But our marriage had quickly turned sour. I realized too late that marriage must be based on something more than a joint interest in flying. Technically, my grounds for divorce had been adultery, but that was only an easy way out. Our differences were much deeper, which was why everything Dale said tended to trigger in me a negative response.

Much to Dale's amazement at the time, I had managed to get the flight school in our divorce settlement. It was his own fault for underestimating me. When it had finally sunk in that he no longer owned Carruthers Aviation, as the school was called then, he merely shrugged and walked out of my life. I'd met him briefly at airports from time to time, but we hadn't seen each other for several years.

Dale reached for the check, but I quickly put my hand over it. "My passengers are paying for this."

"They may not like it if they see two meals on the check."

"They'll never look." I glanced at the total. "They'll expect my own meal to be twice as expensive as this total bill. They won't notice. They wanted to put me up in a Hilton."

"You're operating in classier circles than we used to." His voice was neutral. "By the way, did a kid named Zane Rossiter ever come to you for his commercial training?"

"Yes, he did. I didn't know you were still instructing."

"I'm not, but I got stuck in Whitehorse for a couple of weeks and when this kid came along, I thought, what the hell. Why not? Turned out to be a damn good student, too."

"Yes, he is." Obviously, Zane's account of toning down his exotic appearance must if anything have been understated. Dale didn't even mention it. Back in the seventies, Dale still wore his hair short and called longhaired males sissies. If they cut their hair, they wouldn't have to wear beards in order to prove they were men, he said. And curls! Never, never, never! Dale's own hair was naturally curly and would have been very attractive if he'd let it grow out. He was positively embarrassed by it. I doubted that he had changed his attitudes.

Outside the cafe, we stood awkwardly on the sidewalk. I supposed that Dale had a room at the motel, which still flashed its "Vacancy" sign. I planned to stay there, and my bag was still in the plane. I was trying to think of an excuse to go back to the airport—to go back by myself. I knew what was coming next.

"Robin. I miss you. How about spending the night with me?"

I shook my head.

"Come on, Robin. You used to enjoy it. But I don't suppose you do now, or you'd have gotten married again." I recognized the plaintive tone to his voice: I'd heard it a lot when I'd been married to him. Should I or should I not tell him that the one thing, the only thing, I missed about marriage was sex? But it wasn't enough to get me to make the same mistake again.

"Excuse me. I've got to go back to the airport." I turned away, but Dale reached out and caught my arm. "I know. You left your bags in the plane. I'll go with you and carry them back."

"No, Dale."

"Come on, Robin. Why are you doing this to me? We were married once, remember? No one will pay any attention." His voice had shifted from the hoarse manliness which was his usual way of speaking to a soft, wistful, pleading petition. He told me of long winter nights in the frozen north, of his loneliness, of missing me and wishing he had been a better husband. He told me of his joy at seeing me learn to fly as a young, vibrant girl who loved life, and reminded me of flying trips we had taken together. He reminded me that our love life had been good and said he missed it. He talked all the way down the road, while I unlocked the baggage compartment and retrieved my overnight bag and my flight case, and all the way back to the motel. Stopping in front of the motel, he asked me again, "How about it, Robin?"

He was so convincing. He unlocked a lot of memories. We did have fun together. I'd never really forgotten that, but usually only gave it a passing thought. He had made me remember the good times of our marriage. He was waiting expectantly for an answer. I turned and looked him right in the eye.

"No!" I said very firmly.

He was crestfallen. His tall figure slumped. His expression was incredulous. "Why not?" he wailed.

How could I explain to him? In cowardly fashion, I reverted to side issues. "I don't want to get AIDS."

"Robin!"

"Well, you sleep with all kinds of women. Maybe not AIDS, but there are other sexually transmitted diseases."

"I'll wear a goddam rubber if you want."

"The answer is still 'No'."

He stood and stared at me. I turned away, but he caught my arm again. "Robin. I need to know why."

I took a deep breath and let it out slowly. "All right, Dale, I'll tell you. It's because I don't believe a word you said. If I hadn't conveniently turned up, you'd have found someone else."

I left him there on the sidewalk, his mouth hanging open, speechless. I went into the motel, registered, paid, picked up my bags and walked deliberately to my room. I opened the door, stepped in, closed and firmly locked it. I would not open it if Dale came knocking.

He didn't. I didn't see him again, but was awakened the next morning by the sound of a Beaver on amphibious floats taking off on an instrument flight through the early morning fog.

I went to bed with a feeling of relief, not about my encounter with Dale; I'd settled matters with him years ago. I now realized why I had taken an instant dislike to Clive Hawthorne and had been worrying about Faith. Clive's little-boy desire to please, to make everyone happy, had the same false ring as Dale's pleading. Far from being alarmed by this, I was relieved.

Dale hadn't a mean bone in his body. He was honest — well, usually — his little deceptions not being intended to hurt. He was law-abiding and generous. If he pirated other people's business, it was because it was the norm and he expected it to be done to him. He was just better at it than other people, because he could charm everyone from lonely women to hardened bush pilots with his captivating little stories.

So if Clive did the same thing, why should I be alarmed? I'd misjudged him, and if he made Faith happy, then more power to him. I determined to give him the benefit of the doubt and start being nice to him. Really nice, not merely polite.

With this thought in my head, I settled down to one of the last peaceful nights I would have for some time.

TWELVE

Faith and Clive returned to the airport shortly before noon. They were all smiles as we loaded the airplane and took off. The warm weather following a week of soaking rain had caused the dampness from the ground to permeate the lower atmosphere, producing wispy fog and low cloud early in the morning. By noon, however, the bright sun had burned off the fog, though scattered clouds hung along the mountainsides. The forecast for Exeter was for broken cloud, about six tenths sky cover over the valley, but the ceiling and visibility were good, so I felt I could let down into the valley in visual conditions. I didn't file an instrument flight plan, giving myself more leeway to show my passengers some sights of interest.

Flying east gave an entirely different perspective to the same landscape we had flown over the day before. The warm weather had also made its changes. The major highway across the top of the mountains now showed bare patches, where yesterday it had been covered with packed snow. I didn't envy Zane his drive to and from Vancouver. We spotted an avalanche and circled it in our silent upper world, while tonnes of snow hurtled down a wilderness mountainside.

The forecast was accurate, with fleecy cumulus clouds, their bases about 4000 feet above the valley floor. Faith was thrilled by the spectacle of the pure white clouds sliding by on either side, their shapes constantly changing, but when I turned to Clive, I was amazed to find him manfully trying to control his fear. His body seemed frozen in position, his hands clenched, a pallor showing under his perpetual tan. I turned back to my flying, but as we turned onto a long final for runway 21, I sneaked a quick glance in his direction. He had not changed his position or said a word since we had entered the cloud world.

When I had parked the Bonanza and shut down the engine, Clive opened the door, climbed out onto the wing, looked all around, and heaved a mighty sigh. Only then did he relax. He didn't actually kiss the ground, but he might as well have. Faith, who had admitted at first to being a wee bit nervous, while Clive heartily declared that flying in small planes was perfectly safe, was now bubbling with enthusiasm. Aha, I thought, Mr. Hawthorne, I've found your Achilles heel. I would not exploit it, however. I never like to make fun of people who are afraid of flying. Besides, I had decided that Clive was an all-right guy. Maybe the next time he flew, he would be more relaxed.

On Wednesday and Thursday, Zane flew with Jan in the mornings, always finding a place to stop for lunch, then flew solo in the afternoons. Jan, looking well fed and happy, reported that he was making excellent progress. Thursday evening, Lance Brock turned up early for ground school and asked to see me. He watched Zane enviously, and I could see that his enforced inaction while he toiled in a factory that made mobile homes, was creating anxiety.

"I've just got enough block time left to fly this weekend, and I don't get paid till next Friday. I wondered if you'd let me fly on credit just for next week, so I could come out after work and put in some time."

I adhered to a hard and fast rule that everyone had to pay up every time they flew. If I hadn't held to that rule, I'd have been broke long ago. Students could get "block time" however, by paying larger sums ahead of time, and would then receive a discount. If ever there was a time I would like to have scrubbed this rule, it was now. Lance had shown that when properly motivated, he could learn quite rapidly, and the motivation came from Zane. Zane would finish before Lance, but the shorter the interval between the two of them finishing their course, the more likely it would be that Lance would stick with it.

On the other hand, if I made an exception for one student, I'd have to for others. The margin of profit in this business is narrow. I couldn't afford to extend credit. Lance was not the best of credit risks, either. If he decided to quit before I got my money, I could kiss it good-bye. How could I resolve this dilemma?

Hmm. Maybe Zane could help me out.

"I'm sorry, Lance, but I can't break my rule. It has to be pay as you fly. I can't stay in business otherwise." I saw him open his mouth to protest, but I held up my hand to silence him. "I'd really like to. I think you need to fly as often as possible. I've got an idea. Why don't you ask Zane if he'd take you along instead of flying solo."

I saw the flash of excitement in Lance's eyes. "D'you think he would."

"I've no idea. Why don't you ask him?"

Lance shot out of my office. Moments later, I heard him in earnest conversation with Zane. After a few minutes, Zane hailed me. "Robin, is there any reason why I can't take someone along instead of flying solo?"

"None at all."

"Great! Lance and I will be going out together."

"Okay. Just remember, though, both of you. The pilot in the left seat is pilot in command with all its responsibilities. The one in the right seat is a passenger. That doesn't mean that the passenger can't do any flying, but only with the permission of the PIC, and the PIC is still in charge. Understood?"

They both nodded. They went off to figure out a schedule and reserve a plane.

I had letters to catch up on and stayed in my office while ground school was in session. By the middle of it, Jan's voice had become hoarse, and she complained of a sore throat. I told her to take Friday off. Zane could either fly solo, or I'd get one of my part-time instructors to come in. That problem was solved for me, however, when Ralph Thompson's Twin Comanche rolled up and disgorged three tired but happy travelers. They said they hadn't won anything in Las Vegas, but had a good time anyway. Eve gently ribbed Ralph about having to fly under the instrument hood while she got to look at the gorgeous countryside. Ralph went back out to secure his plane while Terry busied himself with the inevitable paperwork.

The door to the classroom opened and disgorged the ground school students, Zane prominent among them, who headed for the snack bar. Terry dropped his pen and stared.

"*What* is *that?*"

"Terry, mind your manners," I scolded, fighting down a swell of mirth.

"Sorry. *Who* is that?"

"His name is Zane Rossiter, and you are going to fly with him tomorrow." I explained that Zane was a capable commercial student who had been flying with Jan, that Jan was developing laryngitis and would be grounded until she was better, and that Terry should check with her about what his new student needed to work on.

"Okay," his voice was neutral. "But he looks gay. He doesn't look like a pilot."

"You're thinking in stereotypes. Just because he curls his hair doesn't mean he's gay. As a matter of fact, he has a very healthy masculine interest in a couple of attractive young women." I deliberately made my voice stern while I gave this lecture.

Terry surveyed the assembled students again, then asked cautiously, "That isn't Lance Brock, is it? What's he doing here?"

"It is. He is working toward his commercial and you are going to be his instructor. I've done his evaluation flights and tomorrow I'll go over with you what he needs. He won't be flying until Saturday."

"Okay," he replied grudgingly.

"Terry. Don't pre-judge either of them."

He nodded sheepishly. "Sorry," he said.

At noon the next day, Zane and Terry came back from their flight. Zane hadn't taken Terry out to lunch. After Zane had left, I asked, "How'd it go?"

Terry looked up, a broad smile on his face. "Just great! I'd like to have more students like that. He absorbs new things like a sponge and he really tries. I'm sorry about last night. I misjudged him."

That was a relief. Terry was used to being the handsome young bachelor around the place. I'd been worried that he might be jealous and try to make things rough for Zane. Now I would wait and see how he reacted to Lance. If he did well, it would make a good example of his maturity on any evaluation for responsible flying jobs. I was as anxious to see Terry succeed as I was for either of the others.

THIRTEEN

While nearly everyone comes to church on Easter, almost no one does on the following Sunday. Only the most loyal church-goers straggled in on a warm, sunny morning, while their fellow parishioners headed for the golf courses. There was one among the loyal contingent who, quite surprisingly, wasn't there either.

The third reading is from one of the four Gospels. Rather than stepping up to the lectern, the person reading the Gospel does so from the floor, in the midst of the congregation. The Gospel used to be read by a priest or deacon, from the pulpit, giving rise to the term "Gospel side" when speaking of the north side of the church where the pulpit is located. The south side, where the lectern is placed, is called the "Epistle side" because the second reading, the Epistle, is read from the lectern.

Our Bishop, The Right Reverend Michael Staines, was of the modern school and preferred that the Gospel be read by a lay member of the congregation. This had not been done until Douglas arrived, but now it was the way we always did it.

The altar attendant, Lesley Randall-Jones, left his seat in the sanctuary at the beginning of the last verse of the Gradual Hymn. He picked up the Gospel Book, bowed before the altar, turned, and holding the book high over his head, strode down the central aisle to a point about one third of the way along. On Easter Sunday, the altar attendant had been preceded by the crucifer, carrying the processional cross, and by two small boys carrying candles. Today, we did not have such an elaborate Gospel procession.

The Gospeller who would do the reading should have been following close behind Lesley. No one was there. I glanced around the church. Everyone remained glued to their seats. I looked at my leaflet. The third reader for the day was listed as Owen Dunphy.

Owen wouldn't miss something as important as this! Lesley Randall-Jones had turned to face the altar, had opened the Gospel Book to the pre-marked page, and had discovered that he was standing there by himself. His eyes searched the congregation. Owen was nowhere to be seen. In alarm, he looked frantically around for an alternate. The first one his eyes lighted upon was me. We were all standing, facing him. Our eyes met. "Robin, please, come read the Gospel."

I opened my mouth to demur, then thought better of it. Lesley needed someone immediately, and no one else would be any better prepared to read than I was. I stepped out into the aisle, faced Lesley, and remembered to start out with the phrase, "The Lord be with you." While the congregation responded, "And also with you," I said a little prayer asking God to please put the right words into my mouth. He did.

I heard myself say, "The Holy Gospel of our Lord Jesus Christ according to John." While the parishioners chanted in reply, "Glory to you Lord Jesus Christ" and added eight alleluias, to the accompaniment of the organ, I took a quick look at the reading and relaxed. No complicated thoughts, or hard to pronounce names. It was the story of the disciple Thomas, who missed out on Jesus' first post-resurrection appearance, and in anguish declared that he couldn't believe it unless he saw the Lord Himself and put his hand in the wounds. This was granted him, and when he realized that he was in the presence of the risen Christ, he capitulated completely, exclaiming, "My Lord and my God!" Jesus' reply was one that I did not then realize would one day have a powerful significance for me. "Have you believed because you have seen me? Blessed are those who have not seen and yet have come to believe."

The words flowed from my mouth as if I had been practicing them all week. I finished with, "The Gospel of Christ."

"Praise to you Lord Jesus Christ," replied the congregation.

Whew! I got through that all right. I stepped aside, then fell in behind Lesley as he returned to the altar, holding high the Gospel Book. Before the altar, we both bowed deeply. He returned to the sanctuary and I moved across to the south aisle, returned to my row in the pews and climbed across everybody getting back to my seat. Betty Forsythe, who had been sitting beside me, made a small, inconspicuous "okay" sign. I sat down and let out a sigh of relief.

All through the remainder of the service, I could not squelch the nagging thought that if Owen Dunphy was not there, something must have happened to him. As we left the church at the end of the service, we filed out the door and were greeted by Douglas. While Betty picked up Douglas' chasuble, which he had removed, folding it neatly across her arm, I said to Douglas, "I'm worried about Owen. He should have been here to read the Gospel."

"Yes, it is odd, isn't it. He never misses. By the way, you read very well. Thanks for filling in."

I thanked him for the compliment, but returned to my concern over Owen.

"Maybe he hasn't gotten back from his trip," Douglas suggested.

"He'd have called and let us know. But also, when I came by his house this morning, his car was in the driveway."

Douglas stared at me. "He must be ill."

"Too ill to get to the phone and call us. I wonder if he's had a heart attack."

Other people were queuing up behind us. Douglas said, "Meet me in the office in a few minutes."

In the office, Betty took Douglas' alb as he removed it and remarked, "This is getting dirty. I'd better take it home and wash it." Douglas carefully hung up his chasuble and stole. With these housekeeping chores done, he turned to face me.

"I think we ought to go to Owen's house and see if he's all right. Do you ladies want to come with me?"

We said we would. We piled into the Forsythe's Jeep Cherokee, which they had bought to pull a travel trailer across the country, and when they settled here, had kept as a useful camping vehicle. Betty had since gotten a small Honda to run around town in.

Owen lived in one side of an older duplex, set well back from the street and surrounded by flower gardens. A tan Ford Escort, several years old, sat in the carport beside folded lawn chairs and an assortment of cardboard boxes. Gardening tools were stored in a corner of the carport.

The drapes were pulled across all the windows, but from the front step, I could see a lighted lamp showing through a gap between the front window curtains. The front porch light was also lit. When Owen did not answer, we went around to the back door and knocked. Again, we could see through the thin kitchen curtains that the lights were on.

"I don't like this," Douglas said. We tried both doors. They were locked.

Betty suggested, "We could go to the neighbours and see if anyone has a key."

We got no response from the other side of the duplex, but a man mowing his yard next door shut down his mower and told us, "They're not home. They winter in Mexico and won't be back for another week or two."

"Actually, we weren't looking for them," Douglas explained. "We are trying to find out about the man in the other side of the duplex."

The neighbour shrugged. "I don't know him."

"Then you wouldn't know who might have a key?" The man shook his head and Douglas continued. "We think something might have happened to him."

"I can't help you. I'm sorry."

I suggested, "Perhaps the man who runs the office for Owen would have a key. Maybe we could call him. Let me think. Owen told me his name. Elliot - Elliot Truesdale, I think it was."

"You're welcome to use the phone. Come on in. The phone book is in the drawer under the phone."

Douglas looked up the number and dialled. I let out my breath when it became evident that Truesdale was at home, and Douglas began explaining the situation. I hadn't realized how tense I'd become. Douglas hung up.

"Truesdale has a key and will be right over." Douglas thanked our host, and we trooped on back to Owen's duplex.

It took Truesdale about five minutes to get there. He pulled into the driveway, got out of his minivan, and bustled over to the door, searching through a ring full of keys of every size and shape. He tried two before he found the right one, unlocked the door and put the keys back in his pocket. Opening the door, he called, "Owen!" and waited a moment listening for an answer. Not hearing anything, he pushed the door farther open and stepped into the living room of Owen's duplex. He took two steps, stopped in his tracks, turned and staggered back to the door. We caught him as he began to collapse and sat him down on the step. Betty pushed his head down between his knees, but not before we had all seen his face. It was the colour of porridge, and held an expression of stark horror.

As the Forsythes ministered to the stricken man, I slipped away and stepped in the door of the house. The stench of decaying flesh assailed my nostrils in the stifling warmth of the interior. I felt that I had known since we arrived at the house that we would find Owen dead, but I was not prepared for what I saw.

FOURTEEN

I took only a quick look at the bloated body, lying on its back, arms akimbo. Trying to avoid the gruesome sight, I concentrated on other details.

He had been dressed in the brown suit he always wore to church. I had often wondered when it would wear out, or whether he kept getting more suits of the same pattern. I'd been attending St. Matthew's for five years, and could not remember Owen wearing anything else. When he died, he'd been wearing a white shirt, open at the collar, and a red tie hanging loose around his neck. The red tie was also typical, though I couldn't remember for certain whether I'd ever seen him wearing another.

The front of the white shirt showed a circular, dark red stain. The blood had dried out and was beginning to flake off. In the centre of the stain was a small hole.

There were two glasses on the floor, one on either side of the body. The beige carpet had been stained around these glasses, but whatever liquid had been spilled had dried. What the liquid had probably been was revealed by the uncapped whiskey bottle on a table beside the body. There were other items of drinking paraphernalia, but not being an imbiber myself, I did not identify them. It looked very much as if Owen had poured drinks for himself and one other person and had been shot while still holding them.

Nothing else in the room seemed out of place or unusual in any way.

Owen was a neat housekeeper. I remembered from the few times I'd been in this house on church business, that he had a place for everything and didn't like clutter. He often worked on the dining room table, with papers in neat piles and a calculator placed precisely where he could use it easily. The calculator was there, with two pens laid carefully beside it. There were no papers, neat or otherwise.

Controlling a rising tide of nausea with an effort, I backed out of the room. Douglas looked up, questioningly.

"He's been murdered," I said.

"Murdered?"

"Yes. Shot in the chest. He must have had a guest. He'd poured two glasses of whiskey and dropped both of them when he was hit. He's been dead several days."

The man whose house we had called from, had wandered back, curiosity sticking out all over him. After suitable shocked expressions, he offered to call the police and dashed off. We waited silently for several minutes before they arrived. Truesdale gradually got some colour back in his face and we unfolded one of the lawn chairs and got him into it. He was still pretty shaky.

Sergeant Bruce Jameson of the local RCMP detachment was the first on the scene, along with a uniformed constable. Other policemen, uniformed and not, flooded in, some carrying cases of equipment. They strung yellow tape around the house to keep out the curious and set about their well-practiced routines.

After a brief acknowledgment of our presence and a request to stay put, Jameson disappeared into the house. A few minutes latter, we heard familiar voices talking to the policemen in the street. They seemed to be denying entrance to Shirley and Harry Meacham, so Douglas went over, talked to the policemen, and came back with the couple, who were horrified and subdued by the news.

"We were driving past," Shirley explained, "and we saw all the police cars. We were wondering why Owen wasn't in church, but I never imagined that something so awful would have happened to him."

Truesdale, still wrapped in his private anguish, seemed not to notice the newcomers.

Bruce Jameson came back out of the house, pausing to blow his nose heartily. I doubted that he had a cold. I'd like to have gotten the stench out of my nostrils too. He was dressed in a neatly pressed suit of a greyish-blue fabric, a light blue shirt and a conservative striped tie. He was tall and slender, with dark hair combed back and slicked down to his head. He had very intense grey eyes, and it was hard to look into them for any length of time. He knew all of us from the church, and we introduced him to Truesdale, explaining the sequence of events that led to our being there. The uniformed constable was interviewing the neighbour, who had become quite garrulous with self-assumed importance. The constable jotted copious notes. The neighbour could be heard telling the constable that Owen was a strange man and it wasn't surprising that he'd been murdered. Only a few minutes before, he had told us that he didn't know Owen. The neighbours in between were away and weren't expected back for a while. No, he hadn't heard any shots. He was sure he would have; his hearing was quite keen. It must have happened when he was out. He'd ask his wife if she heard anything. There was no use talking to the people on the other side of Owen's duplex, separated from his by a seemingly impenetrable hedge. Those people were old, were both deaf as posts, and wouldn't answer the door unless they knew you were coming. Oh yes, they had a phone, but you had to let it ring a long time before they answered it. They were both arthritic and couldn't get around very fast.

"When did you last see Dunphy?" Jameson asked, addressing the whole group of us.

"Last Sunday in church," Douglas, Betty and I all responded.

"We saw him at Compline last Sunday night," the Meachams added.

"Where was that?" Jameson evidently didn't know that Compline was a church service, not a place.

"At the church," Shirley said.

"I mean, where is this Compline."

"Not where but what," Douglas corrected. "Compline is the evening service. We hold it on Sundays, in the church."

"I see. You're sure he was there?"

参照

"He was not only there, he led the service," Harry volunteered.

"Oh? Was he a minister?"

"He wasn't a priest, if that's what you mean," Douglas explained. "However, all members of the church are called to minister to others. In that way, he was a minister."

Jameson seemed uninterested in the nuances of church life. He turned to Elliot Truesdale. "You worked for Dunphy? What sort of a job?"

"Accounting. Owen Dunphy Accounting, Ltd."

"Are you an accountant?"

"Yes. I'm the office manager." Truesdale's voice edged upward toward hysteria.

"Take it easy, sir. I understand that you found him and it wasn't a pretty sight, but we've got to get a bit of background information from you. How long have you worked for him?"

"Since he started the business four years ago." Truesdale took three deep breaths and made an effort to sit up straight.

"Then you know him pretty well."

"Not personally. But I know the business inside out."

"When did you last see him?"

"Not since last Saturday."

"A week ago?"

"That's right. He came into the office Saturday morning. We aren't open on Saturdays but I had some work to catch up on so I was there."

"Why did he come in?"

"He often did. He never stopped working. He said he wanted to take some files that there was some problem with home and work on them."

"Do you know what files?" Jameson's questioning was calm and patient; Truesdale gradually relaxed his clenched hands and sat up more vertically in the lawn chair.

"No. He just went to the room where the filing cabinets are and got them out. I didn't notice."

"I thought everything was done with computers," I interjected.

"It is. But Owen was adamant about having everything on paper to back up the computer data, in case anything was accidentally erased. He preferred to work with the printed data, anyway. He wasn't totally comfortable with computers himself, even though he based his business on computerized procedures."

Jameson turned toward me, his brow furrowed. "What do *you* know about Dunphy's business?"

I explained, "He cornered me one day recently and I couldn't get away before I had listened to the complete history of his business."

Truesdale actually smiled.

Jameson turned back to Truesdale and shot a question at him. "If you're so close to him in his work and run his office, how come you didn't notice that he wasn't there for a whole week?"

Truesdale pulled his slight frame erect and answered in a supercilious voice, "Because he was going on a trip. I didn't expect him back until tomorrow."

Jameson drew out the entire story of Owen's proposed selling trip. "And he wouldn't have contacted you at any time during the week?"

"Not if everything went well."

I butted in again. "He wasn't going to leave until later than he had originally planned."

Truesdale gave me a startled glance. Jameson skewered me with his piercing grey eyes, bending his tall, slender frame toward me. "Explain, please, Mrs. Carruthers."

"He was going to leave Sunday after the 10:30 service, but he put off his trip so that he could lead Compline. He was apparently going to start out Monday morning. Then he came across something fishy in some of the accounts his firm was working on, so he delayed his trip again in order to look into it. That's probably what he was doing in the office Saturday, picking up the files on those accounts."

Truesdale was staring at me in open-mouthed astonishment, his face now suffused with blood. Jameson turned back to him. "Is that correct?"

"I never heard anything like that! He said he had some problem accounts to work on, which wasn't unusual."

"Where'd you get this information?" Jameson demanded of me.

"Actually, I got it second-hand. He was talking about it as he left church Sunday, and some friends of mine told me about it at coffee hour."

"That's right, though," Harry Meacham stated. "He was talking about it at Compline Sunday night." Harry turned toward Truesdale. "If it's news to you, it's probably because he didn't realize what he was on to until he'd gone over the files."

"Hold it," Jameson said. "Let's get everything in order here. Mr. Meacham, did you personally hear Dunphy talking about this?" I had noticed during a previous run-in with Jameson, that he referred to dead people by their last names only, but when addressing a live one, he would use the appropriate formal salutation.

"Yes."

"I did too," Shirley chimed in.

"Tell me what he said."

Shirley and Harry exchanged glances. It was Harry who spoke.

"He was tickled pink. He'd uncovered some form of financial trickery. He said he had been suspicious the first time he saw it, about a month ago, wasn't it?" He looked at Shirley who nodded. "Then he said he'd found another incident of the same thing the previous week, and then another, I assume, just a day or so earlier. After the third incident, he knew he was on to something criminal. He said that he was going to spend three days sorting it all out. Then he was going to take the information to a bank that had something to do with it and to Revenue Canada. Is that right?" He asked this last question of Shirley, who nodded.

Jameson turned to me. "Is this what you heard?"

"I didn't hear him say it. I only know what I heard second-hand."

Turning to Douglas, Jameson asked, "Do you know anything about this?"

"No. I wasn't there Sunday night. That's why Owen was taking Compline that night. I took a few days off after Easter, and Betty and I were out of town visiting friends."

"Who else knew about this?"

"About half the people in church on Easter Sunday, I'd guess," I remarked facetiously.

"And everyone at Compline," Harry added.

"Explain," Jameson demanded of me.

"Owen had a loud voice and didn't mind who heard him. I avoided talking to him on the way out of church, because I could tell by the tone of his voice that he was ranting on about something. I tend to turn my mind off on those occasions, but anyone near him who cared to listen could have heard."

"Who told you?"

"Penny Farnham and Paul St. Cyr." Jameson knew both of them so I didn't identify them any further. He turned to the Meachams.

"Who heard him say this at the evening service?"

"Let's see." Shirley searched her memory. "Several members of our Bible study group. Owen asked them all to come." She started to name them, when another voice joined in.

"And me."

"And who are you, sir?"

"Don Urquhart. I run The Veggie Farm."

Jameson nodded. "Anyone else?"

Don asked, "Did anyone mention Faith?" We shook our heads. We had a tendency to forget her, she was so quiet and retiring. "Faith LaBounty," Don explained.

"How about Clive Hawthorne," I asked. "Where Faith goes these days, there also goes Clive."

"He came to pick her up. He was waiting at the door, wasn't he, Harry?"

"Yes, I think so."

A constable who was scribbling names asked for spellings. As he did so, Jameson noticed another person who had joined the group. "Hello, Miss Farnham. I understand that you overheard Owen Dunphy saying he had found something wrong with some accounts."

She smiled at him. "Yes, that's right."

"And that he was going to stick around for three days going over the accounts."

"Uh, something like that. What's happened anyway. Don and I were sidespersons and while we were in the office counting the collection, we heard you talking about going out to Owen's house to see what had happened to him, so we decided to come along ourselves." She addressed the question to Douglas, but he deferred to Jameson.

"Owen Dunphy has been murdered, Miss Farnham." Penny gasped and there a brief expletive from Don, who then glanced toward Douglas and put his hand over his mouth as if to push the word back in. Douglas paid no attention.

Harry explained, "I believe that what Owen said was that he was going to take three days to go over the records, compile his evidence, and then go to the authorities with it.

"Miss Farnham?" Jameson's tone was friendly and coaxing. She frowned, then nodded. "I guess that's right."

"So if he started working on it on Monday, he would have been done on Wednesday?" The Meachams and Don all nodded.

Penny frowned, concentrating. "No, he said he wasn't coming to coffee after church because he was going home to start working on it."

"So that meant he'd be done on Tuesday."

"I don't know," Harry responded thoughtfully, looking around at the others. After some hesitation, everyone nodded.

I said, "He got the files on Saturday. If it took him three days to go over them, he'd be finished Monday."

"And go to the bank on Tuesday, when they'd be open after the holiday?" Jameson asked. We all nodded again.

Jameson continued, directing the next question to Harry, "Why the bank?"

Penny interjected, "I think it was because he didn't know the name of the person or people who were doing whatever it was, but the bank would know, and they could notify the police."

"What bank?"

We all shook our heads.

"Presumably it had something to do with taxes, since he was also going to Revenue Canada. Did he say anything about taxes?"

"Everything to do with money is about taxes," Don Urquhart expostulated forcefully. A flicker of a smile crossed Jameson's face.

"So, since the bank didn't come to us," Jameson mused, "and Revenue Canada didn't come to us, it would seem that Dunphy was killed sometime before Tuesday."

"Sometime in the evening," I said. "The drapes were closed, the lights were on and so was the heat."

Jameson gave me a little bow. "Elementary, my dear Watson." My face turned brick red. I was saved further embarrassment by the fact that a uniformed constable was standing impatiently at Jameson's elbow, a small brown notebook in his hand, carefully opened to a page about one fourth of the way through. It was a pocket diary, I realized.

"Corporal Smith thought you ought to see this right away. It was in the dead man's inner jacket pocket."

They moved a few paces from us while Jameson perused the entry in the diary. Then he spun on his heel, covering the distance back to our group in two long strides, eyeing us like a teacher with an unruly group of schoolchildren. Watching our faces, he recited, "'Aha! I've got the culprit! Wait till tomorrow!'" He let it sink in, then went on, "It's not written on a specific day, but scrawled

114

across the line for the whole week. I think we can assume that 'tomorrow' was Tuesday. So I'll want to know where each of you was on Monday night.

FIFTEEN

I started off. "I was in Vancouver on a charter flight. I flew Faith LaBounty and Clive Hawthorne down there Monday afternoon, stayed the night at a motel near Vancouver East Airport, and flew them back on Tuesday. We got back in the early afternoon. I can give you precise times for everything if you need them."

"These people you flew down there; did they stay at the same motel?"

"No. I don't know exactly where they stayed overnight. They said they were going to stay with friends. On Tuesday morning, they went to the Australian Consulate. They were planning a trip to Australia."

"I see. I'll want more details from you, but that's enough for now. You, sir, were out of town?" He addressed this inquiry to Douglas.

"Yes. Betty and I were visiting friends in Calgary. I can give you their names and address."

"I'll get that later." He turned expectantly toward the Meachams.

"We went out to the new seafood place in the mall. Don went with us," Shirley responded.

"No, that was Sunday after Compline," Harry corrected her. "Wasn't it, Don?"

"Let's see. Yeah, you're right. Owen invited everyone out to his place for drinks, but we were going to the seafood place, so we declined."

"You say Dunphy invited everyone to his place? Did anyone take him up on it?"

Don pondered for a moment. "I don't think so. Faith said she had to go home and pack for her trip the next day. Clive took her home."

Jameson turned back to the Meachams. "So where were you on Monday evening?"

"We were at home all evening on Monday, I guess," Harry replied.

"Yes, that's right," Shirley agreed.

"I was at home, alone." Penny had been out with Zane every other night in the week, but since he was in Vancouver on Monday night, it was the one time she had been left alone.

"I was in my office at my veggie stand," Don explained. "I don't suppose I can prove that I stayed there, but I think my wife would have noticed if I'd come back over to the house and taken the pickup."

"Mr. Truesdale?" Jameson prodded.

Truesdale turned belligerent. "I was at home—*with* my wife. I resent your implication that I killed Owen."

Jameson held up a hand and waved it from side to side. "Please don't take offence. I'm not accusing you. I just need to gather all the information I can." Truesdale was not mollified. He sat rigidly in the lawn chair, his mouth formed into a pout, defiance and self-pity struggling for supremacy.

"I'll be around to see each one of you to get more details," Jameson went on. "Mrs. Carruthers, are you going to be out at the airport this afternoon?"

"Yes, later on."

"I suggest that the rest of you stay at your homes until we come around, if you possibly can. Mr. Truesdale, do you feel up to driving home or would you rather have someone take you?"

Truesdale arose from his chair, pulled his slender frame up to his full five feet seven, and snapped at Jameson, "I am perfectly capable of taking care of myself."

117

"Good. You may all leave now." We started to move away when he called to us again. "Do any of you know of any other reason someone might want Dunphy dead?"

We hesitated, then something nagged at my memory. "Owen told me about someone who was embezzling from his brother. It was several years ago, up in Kluane Junction. His brother had a mining company. The wife of one of the mine managers was acting as bookkeeper. She stole from the company. Owen got the goods on her, she was arrested, and the mine manager was fired."

"Did he tell you the name of this person?"

"The mine manager was named Sam Kruse, I think. I don't believe he told me the wife's name."

"Anything else?"

We all shook our heads. Douglas asked, "Do you need any information about Owen? We have the name of his brother in the Yukon."

"No. It was all in a notebook in his desk. Neat guy. Seemed to keep his papers in order. That always helps."

"Speaking of papers," I remarked, "Owen usually worked on his dining room table. If he took three folders home from the office, where were they?"

Jameson paused a moment, as if about to answer me, then turned and walked away. I saw Truesdale frowning in my direction and asked him, "What would these files look like? I didn't see anything in that room."

Truesdale paused for a few seconds, then sagging back into a state of lethargy, responded. "They would be ordinary manila folders, unless the file was a big one. Then they'd be in an accordion-style brown folder. Owen was pretty old-fashioned."

"How were they filed? Could you tell what folders are missing?"

"They're filed alphabetically. It depends on whether Owen put a marker in the slot where he'd taken the file out. If not, you couldn't tell if the file was missing."

"But you must have an index."

"Not with the files."

"The same information is in the computers, isn't it?"

"It should be."

Douglas had been following the discussion with interest. He, Betty, Truesdale and I formed a tight little group on the driveway, the others having drifted off. "Did Owen have a computer at home?"

"Yes, and it's connected to the office computers, but he wasn't completely comfortable with computers himself. He knew their value, but for his own purposes, he liked things on paper."

I said, "I can understand that. I feel the same way myself."

Douglas got us back on the subject. "Assuming that his killer took the files, I wonder whether he would have tried to erase the data from the computer. Could he have done that?"

A look of horror spread over Truesdale's face. "I hope not! If that happened, we'd have no record at all of an entire company's accounts."

"Exactly."

"What would we tell the customer?" Truesdale wailed.

"Before you could tell the customer anything, you'd have to figure out who the customer was," I reminded him. "Which brings us back to my question about having an index. Surely, you have some way of telling what files are in the computer; a numbering system or something."

"I — I don't know. There are account numbers that we use to pull up a file, but when I want one, I usually enter the name of the account to retrieve it."

"The computer operators who do all the entries must know. How do they retrieve the file they want?"

"By name usually."

"But there must be a cross reference."

"Yes, but I'm not sure you could go to the computer and ask it if any file was missing." An appalled expression spread over his face as the enormity of the situation sank in.

I said, "Then you might have to go to the printed files and try to match one to each file in the computer to find the three that are gone."

"Oh, no! There are thousands of them!"

"Or wait until the company calls you up and wants to know what you're doing with their account."

From the expression of dismay on Truesdale's face, I could tell that this option was even worse.

"I think we should go," Douglas said. Turning toward Truedale, he asked in a kindly voice, "Are you sure you don't want us to take you home?"

"No. I'm all right. Thanks anyway."

He got in his minivan and backed carefully out of the driveway.

"I wonder," I said to nobody in particular, "how easy it would be to completely wipe out an entire record."

"From what I've heard some people say," Betty responded with feeling, "as easy as having a cat walk across the keyboard."

We drove back to the church so that I could retrieve my Ford Ranger pickup truck, which had replaced the old station wagon I had driven for years.

"I'll wait until the police have notified Owen's brother, then call him. I think his name is Garrick Dunphy. I'm sure he's still in Kluane Junction," Douglas mused, as if planning the rest of his day out loud. "I wonder when the police will come around to the rectory?"

"It doesn't make much difference," Betty replied. "We'll be there. Probably everyone in the parish will call and you'll never get off the phone."

"Probably."

They let me off and drove away. I went out to the flight school. Lance was in the circuit, solo, practicing takeoffs and landings. He was doing well, as he could when he wanted to. He was making nice landings, right on the button, and his transition from the landing to the take-off phase was smooth, not rushed, but without tying up the runway unnecessarily, either. Good. I wouldn't have to worry about him for a while yet.

Zane was shut up in the ground school room, where Jan had him writing a practice test to see if he was ready for the real one. She had given him special tutoring, since he was already way ahead of his ground school classmates, and he had completed the entire ground school course. His flying had reached the point, Jan told me, where he could have passed the flight test right now. He still needed many more hours of dual instruction in order to satisfy the requirements, so Jan would be able to work on extras beyond the basic curriculum.

Not much else was going on. The weather had turned sour again; overcast with gusty winds. It was not a good day for pleasure flying.

I stopped in front of Gayla's desk and told her, "A man from the RCMP will be out here sometime this afternoon to see me. I'll be in my office."

I could see the question in her eyes, but noting that I did not seem inclined to comment further, she didn't let it leave her lips. I felt acutely disinclined to discuss Owen's death with anyone else. I busied myself with other work, trying to forget the gruesome sight of his very long-dead body.

About an hour later, Gayla poked her head into my office. "Garth Hughes is on the line."

Garth, who ran a flight school in Pine Hill and had refused to fly with Lance Brock, was a long-time rival who had proffered his friendship and cooperation to me only the previous summer. I had been glad to accept. I much preferred to get along well with others in the business.

"Hello, Robin. I hear that Brock is back with you again. How's he doing?"

"Pretty well so far. He and another student started their commercial training at the same time and there's a sort of rivalry. It's keeping Lance on his toes."

"Good. Hey, what I called about is that I'm considering upgrading my training aircraft, and I can't decide what to get. The old 150s and 152s are falling apart, and neither Cessna nor Piper is making anything new. What are you doing? Still hanging on, or thinking of replacing yours?"

"I've been thinking about it, but I don't know what to get. The trouble is, if you want to change, you've got to get all new airplanes at the same time. You can't just replace one at a time any more. And you can't have two kinds of trainers. They've all got to be one type."

"Yeah, and with the 150s and 152s, the students can transition up to 172s and 182s easily. Damn! I wish Cessna was still building them."

"Me too. Have you looked at anything else?"

"I looked at this Canadian-built composite, but I'm not sure I'd care for it. I know composites are the new thing, but the plane looks sort of airy-fairy. It looks like a toy. I'm not sure that students would go for it."

"I'd been thinking of getting some data on those Czech trainers. They have a sort of macho look about them, and the company has been in business for years and is going to be there for lots more."

"Yeah, but they're foreign. You wouldn't know whether you could get parts. Besides, I like high-wing planes, though they don't seem to build them any more."

"High-wings are better for training, all right. The student can see more of the ground on cross-country flights."

"They're also bloody better for mountain flying for the same reason!" Garth should know. He'd done a lot of flying over our province's inhospitable terrain. "One thing I've been thinking; all the schools in this area should probably go to the same type of trainer. Otherwise, it would mean a lot longer checkout when people went from one school to another and that would hurt business."

"What did you have in mind?"

"I wondered if you and the other operators in this neck of the woods would like to get together with me and invite some of these outfits to come and demonstrate their planes. Then we could make a group decision as to what we're going to change over to."

"Sounds like a good idea."

"Okay, I'll get in touch with the others. Maybe we could get together somewhere for a meeting."

"Fine with me. I don't have anything else on the agenda right now."

"I'll set it up and get back to you. Say, I heard you had a murder over there in Exeter. Know anything about it?"

I paused a moment before I replied guardedly, "Yes, I know something about it. But how did *you* know?"

Garth chuckled. "News travels fast."

"I guess!"

Jameson was waiting for me when I hung up the phone. I invited him into the office. The constable with him took out a notebook and carefully recorded the times and places I listed.

"You went right to this motel as soon as you got to the airport?" Jameson asked.

"I had the plane serviced first. Then I had dinner with another pilot at the cafe in the motel. I have all the receipts."

"What was the name of the other pilot?"

"Dale Carruthers."

Jameson jerked his head up. "A relative?"

"Yes."

"What relationship?"

"My ex-husband."

He gave a little smirk. "And you say you spent the night at this motel by yourself?"

"Yes, I did!" I could feel my face redden and my skin get hot.

After a short pause, Jameson asked, "You don't know for sure where these other people went?"

"No. You'll have to ask them."

"Their names were mentioned as being at church on Sunday night. Are they regular members?"

Faith is. Clive Hawthorne isn't and I don't think he was at the service. I think he came by to pick up Faith."

"They're good friends, then?"

"They're going to be married, so I guess they'd better be good friends."

Jameson smiled at that. "I don't suppose they'd like me asking them if they spent the night together, either."

"I don't suppose they would. Faith is a widowed older lady, with emphasis on the lady. She wouldn't do anything improper, including, if you've got her on your list of suspects, plugging Owen in the chest with a gun.

SIXTEEN

Just before Compline that evening, Douglas told me that he would meet Garrick Dunphy as he arrived on the last flight from Vancouver at about nine o'clock. Would I like to come along in case Dunphy had any questions about the finding of his brother's body? I agreed to go.

Douglas had called Kluane Junction, had gotten Mrs. Dunphy who told him that her husband had already left for Exeter. When Dunphy called home from Vancouver while waiting for his flight to Exeter, his wife told him of Douglas' call and he had phoned. Douglas promised to meet him and to help with any arrangements that might be needed in Exeter. Garrick Dunphy, it seemed, possessed the same gift for order and organization as Owen. He had already made reservations for a motel room and a rental car. He needed nothing more.

Garrick Dunphy showed little resemblance to his older brother, and I would not have picked him out. He identified us, however, since Douglas was wearing his clerical collar. We had noticed Jameson and another plain-clothes policeman standing unobtrusively at one side of the waiting room. As soon as we greeted Dunphy, they moved in.

"Excuse us. We need to talk to Mr. Dunphy first."

"You can talk to me here, can't you? I asked these people to meet me because I want to discuss things with them. Reverend Forsythe was my brother's priest."

"Okay. We'll go into the airport manager's office." Jameson turned toward us. "You can wait out here."

We waited nearly half an hour, and when Garrick emerged from the meeting, he was greeted by a contingent of reporters who had been alerted to his arrival. He shouldered his way past, paying them no attention, and said to us, "Let's get out of here. Where can we go?"

"We can go to the rectory. Perhaps the reporters will think you're staying there and go away."

"I doubt it. However, we'll cross that bridge when we come to it."

At the rectory, he listened to the full story of Owen's planned trip, his delayed departure, his boast about having uncovered fraud in some of the accounts he handled, his failure to appear in church, and our subsequent trip to his house to find out what was wrong.

"You say that you think he'd been dead for several days?" he asked me.

"Yes. The police have decided that it must have happened Monday night."

Garrick nodded and sat for a few minutes with his chin in his hand, a scowl creasing his heavy brows. There was a note of agony in his voice when he said, "They say I have to identify the body. I can't get out of it. I have to do that first thing in the morning."

We murmured sympathetic comments. It had been bad enough for me, just the one quick sight of the bloated face. I didn't envy this man. I wondered whether the cold storage would fully eliminate the smell of decaying flesh. I hoped so.

"You know, I'm not surprised that this happened to my brother. He had an absolute talent for nosing out anything that wasn't quite right in a company's books. He wasn't bashful about it either. Did he ever tell you that he'd uncovered an employee who was embezzling from me?"

"Yes, he did," I answered. "Might these people still hold a grudge?"

"They probably do. Sam Kruse said some pretty nasty things, but no one really believed him. Gladys Kruse called Owen some dirty names and spat at him after he had testified against her. But I can't see them coming down here and killing him."

"But his testimony convicted her?"

"Yes. He hadn't left any holes for her to squeeze out through. I'd only had a vague suspicion. I can look at a handful of rocks and tell you what's in them, but accounting is way out of my realm." He stared at the palms of his work-worn hands.

"I understand that's why Owen started his business. Lots of people like you had that problem."

"Yes, that's what happened, all right." He sighed. "Well, I guess I'd better brave the reporters and make my way to my motel. Thanks a lot for your help and your condolences. It's nice to know I've got friends here. Reverend, I'll come to the church tomorrow to talk about…" He couldn't get the words out. Douglas laid a hand on his arm.

"I'll be expecting you."

On mornings when there wasn't much going on at the flight school, I often went to morning prayer in the church. There were usually only a few people present. On Monday, besides Douglas and myself, the only other person present when I arrived was an elderly man who puttered around the church weeding the flower borders, raking leaves, or shovelling off the occasional winter snowfall. We were blessed with mild winters in this interior valley, located in the "rain shadow" of the coastal mountains. Our climate was semi-arid, but though our Chamber of Commerce tried to convince people that it never snowed in Exeter, we did have the occasional covering of white stuff.

Right at eight, as we were about to begin, Garrick Dunphy stuck his head in the door looking uncertain. "Come in, come in," Douglas welcomed him. "We're glad to have you with us this morning."

I supplied Garrick with a small printed program of the morning prayer service and a *Book of Alternative Services*, out of which we would read the Psalms. He thanked me and sat down beside me. During the prayers for members of the parish, there was a special one for the repose of the soul of Owen Dunphy. A candle on the altar, which would burn for eight days, had been lighted in his memory. Douglas prayed also for Garrick and for other members of Owen's family. A sob escaped Garrick's lips, and I put an arm around him. I liked this rather forceful, competent man, who seemed to have such a soft side and a real love for his brother.

After the service, Garrick told Douglas, apologetically, that he had been talking that morning to other relatives back east, and that it had been decided to hold Owen's funeral in Kitchener, Ontario, the family home. It would be in the church Owen had attended as a boy, where he had been a server and a member of the boys' choir.

"Of course, of course," Douglas assured him. "I wonder, though, if you would mind if we had a memorial service for him here. He has been in this parish for four years and has many friends here. His employees might also want to come."

"That would be quite all right with me. I'm glad you want to. Now I have to go identify Owen's body. I wanted some spiritual help before the ordeal, so I came here. The morning prayer session has steadied me."

"Would you like me to come with you?" Douglas asked.

"No thank you, but I appreciate your offer. I'll be all right. The police want to talk to me afterward."

"Feel free to come to the church at any time," Douglas invited.

"Thanks. I may take you up on that."

"Robin," Douglas said to me after Garrick Dunphy had left, "how about going with me to Owen's place of business? I want to convey our sympathy to his employees and to invite them to a memorial service. I think that the time will depend on when the office workers can come. His other friends here were mainly older folk whose schedules aren't so rigid." He grinned at me. "Perhaps with your logical business mind, you'll pick up something of interest there."

I had previously worked out the solution to another mystery in the parish, and had been known as "Our super-sleuth" ever since. I agreed to go with him, and we walked the short distance to where Owen's office was located.

The office occupied most of the basement area of a professional building, but there was no impression of working in a basement. To reach the private entrance we went down a short flight of broad, well-lit stairs and through a large glass door. We found ourselves in a small anteroom with only three chairs. It was obviously not a place where clients waited. It was, however, tastefully decorated in muted colours, with potted plants and a small table with a few trade publications attractively displayed. Neatly folded and laid on a small stand was the current day's business section from the Toronto Globe and Mail.

Behind an enclosed counter, a velvet-voiced receptionist was answering a welter of incoming calls in a calm, detached manner. We had the impression that the calls were from frantic clients wanting to know what was happening to their records. The receptionist had things well in hand, reassuring, explaining, taking names and phone numbers, but skilfully avoiding giving out any information. She was a real pro, and I chalked up another mark on the plus side for Owen's business.

Not all was milk and honey, we were to find as we were admitted to the inner sanctum. The room itself was quite pleasant. The walls of a light peach colour radiated warmth and light under the off-white glow of the new type of fluorescent bulbs that soften the deadly white glare of the old style. The accents in the decor were of a creamy light brown. Screens separating the cubicles where the computer operators worked were of a pale beige. Even with the limited outside light coming through small windows high on the walls, the room had a light, warm appearance.

There were quite a few cubicles. It was obvious that each operator had a private workspace all their own and were allowed to arrange the furniture, the computer components, and any private decorations to suit themselves. Most displayed photos propped on the desks or hung from the partition. Some housed vases of flowers, real or artificial. Through a sliding glass door, we could see a neat, attractive canteen.

Owen's desire to hold onto competent employees obviously did not stop with paying them a good salary. He had made their work space comfortable and inviting.

A grey-haired lady, her full-figured body evidently reined in by Wonderbra's latest in foundation garments so that she could wear the clinging jersey dress of a discrete navy blue, was passing from one cubicle to another, stopping to pat a shoulder here, give a little hug and an encouraging word there, obviously trying to keep the wheels of industry turning during a time of crisis.

But into that world of calm efficiency and attractive ambiance, the high-pitched, angry voice of Elliot Truesdale cut like a knife. We couldn't see him, but through the glass in the upper half of the door to his office, we could see a tall, brassy-looking woman whose thin face was plastered with makeup. Her weight rested on one slender leg, the other foot in its high-heeled pump was crossed in front. The knuckles of her left hand pressed on a bony hip. Her right hand was clenched into a fist on which she leaned as she glared across Truesdale's desk.

"I don't have to take this crap from you," she snarled, her lower lip thrust out belligerently. "I'll quit!"

"You don't have to quit. You've been fired!"

"Since when?" The snarl dissolved into a slack-jawed look of dismay.

"Since right now."

"You can't do that. You have to give me a month's notice."

"I don't think so. You haven't been here for even a month yet."

"Look, you goddamn little pencil pusher," she leaned over the desk, waves of black hair falling forward to obscure her face, "I'll take you to court. You can't do this to me. I've busted my butt to get here on time every day, and I've done all the work I was supposed to do."

"You've also parked your brains at the door."

"What's that supposed to mean, you little creep?"

I could imagine Truesdale pulling himself up to his full height. He replied slowly, unctuously, emphasizing each word. "You have sat at the reception desk since Tuesday, receiving calls from businesses that Owen had appointments with asking why he hadn't showed up, and all you've told them was that you didn't make his appointments."

"So what? That's what he told me to say."

"But anybody with any common sense would have realized before the week was out that there was something wrong if he never showed up for any of his appointments and didn't call in to give you any instructions. I've been wondering all night how come no one noticed that he wasn't keeping his appointments, and then I find out you've been shunting all those calls off to the trash heap."

"It wasn't my job to keep track of his appointments. In fact, he told me not to."

"But if you had any brains, or any interest in the good of the business, you'd have noticed something was wrong."

"You can't get away with insulting me like that. And you've got to give me a month's notice."

"No I don't. You probably cost us thousands of dollars worth of business already, and I'm not going to let you cost us any more."

"How d'you figure that?"

"You've probably lost us a bunch of clients, and damaged our reputation. If we kept you on, I'd be afraid you'd damage us even more."

She drew herself up to her full height. With the addition of her spiky heels, she towered over the now-standing Truesdale. "You're damn r..." she started to shout, then thought better of it. She tossed her long hair back away from her face, said, "You can talk to my lawyer," spun on her high heel, almost losing her balance as she did so, which ruined the effect of her haughty exit.

131

Truesdale walked around his desk to watch her leave. He saw us, blushed and came out to apologize. "She was our receptionist. We just hired her to replace Kari, who had gone on maternity leave." He turned toward the girl at the desk. As we followed his glance, I noticed for the first time that the dulcet tones were coming from a young woman who was exceedingly pregnant. "Kari said she'd fill in until we could find someone else. She's expecting the baby in a couple of weeks."

I remarked, "You could never replace that one, from what I've heard."

"I know," Truesdale sighed. "We weren't completely satisfied with this new girl, but we couldn't find anyone better. Now we have to start all over again."

"It was nice of — Kari, did you say her name was? — to come back and fill in for you," Douglas remarked.

"Yes indeed. Also Madge." He looked toward the motherly lady still circulating among the other workers. "She just recently retired, but she offered to come back and help. She spells Kari at the switchboard."

"I suspect," said Douglas, "that those two will soon have everything back on track."

"I hope so," Truesdale sighed. "What brings you here, Reverend?"

"We're hoping to have a memorial service for Owen Dunphy, and wanted to know whether you and the other employees would like to come. If so, what would be a good time for you?"

"That's nice of you. I think we could just shut down the office for an afternoon and all go to it." He turned toward the room and called out, "Madge."

The lady in the blue jersey dress came over. "Yes, Mr. Truesdale?"

"Madge, I'd like you to meet Reverend Forsythe of Owen's church." He turned toward me. "I'm sorry, I don't know your name, but I remember you were at Owen's house yesterday."

"I'm Robin Carruthers."

Madge acknowledged the introductions and glanced toward Elliot Truesdale expectantly.

"Madge, I'd like you to show these people around and let them meet the employees. Reverend Forsythe wants to invite us all to a memorial service for Owen. Would you set it up with him? I think we should shut down for an afternoon and go en masse. Now, if you'll excuse me…" He sidled off toward his office.

"I'll see what I can arrange." As Truesdale scurried off, Madge turned toward Douglas, raised her eyebrows, and asked, "No funeral?"

"There will be a funeral at his family home in Kitchener," Douglas explained.

"Oh, I see."

"This is an impressive set-up, I must say," Douglas remarked, his gaze sweeping the room. "Were most of the employees happy working here?"

"Yes, they were. Mr. Dunphy did everything he could to make it a pleasant working environment. And he paid well. His theory was that he needed very competent people, and he needed them to stay on. Each person here handles a particular group of accounts, mostly from businesses all in the same field. They get to know the client, not personally, of course, but through the work they did. That way there was a continuity that couldn't be achieved if someone new was always working on the account. And since they handled similar accounts, they became specialists in the needs of businesses in that industry, and could spot things, or make suggestions. In order to do that, people needed to be on the job for extended periods of time. He didn't want employees to just come and go. So when he found someone who could do the work, he tried to hold onto them."

Somehow this didn't square with my knowledge of Owen's personality. I asked, "How did he get along personally with his employees?"

"He didn't have much personal contact. He was rather aloof, and it was hard to get to know him, but I think that in itself was probably an advantage."

"I expect so."

"Actually," Madge confided, "I don't think Mr. Dunphy would have been a very congenial companion away from work. He wasn't my cup of tea, anyway. But he was always very polite. He gave everyone credit for things they'd done, was open to suggestions, and considerate when anyone had a problem."

I noticed one curly-haired young man, his rosy cheeks and full lips showing a hint of makeup, in one of the cubicles. Thumbtacked to the partition was a picture of another young man. When I realized that I had instantly categorized him as gay, I kicked myself for falling into the same trap that had ensnared Terry when he first spotted Zane. Then I saw a second picture, one showing the two young men embracing each other. I was certain that my instant reaction had been correct. I thought that Owen must be very successful at separating his business and personal lives. Also that he could, as Douglas had pointed out, adhere rigidly to archaic religious beliefs, yet be a forward-looking modern businessman. He had shown an adamant dislike of homosexuals, yet here was a youth who by appearances was undoubtedly gay and was not hiding it. As an employer, it would seem that Owen judged people only on their capability in doing their work.

"The employees seem pretty upset," I remarked.

"Yes. But that is partly worry about the future of their jobs. I've been trying to reassure them."

"You think the business will continue, then."

"I think so. Of course it now belongs to the brother. Or at least I assume so. But he sent word, via Elliot, that things should go on as before."

"Will he have Mr. Truesdale continue to run it?"

"Umm. I think he'll have to get someone to replace Mr. Dunphy. I shouldn't say this, but I don't think Elliot could keep the business going. He's good at his job, but he wouldn't be good at Mr. Dunphy's job."

"Which was…?"

"Trouble-shooting. And selling. Elliot can handle things just fine as long as nothing happens. But he can't sell the service. And he'd never have spotted whatever it was that Mr. Dunphy found."

"Which may be just as well for him," Douglas commented.

Madge gasped and her eyebrows shot up as the implication sank in. "You have a point there," she conceded.

Something that Madge said had struck me as important. "You say that individual workers had a group of accounts that they always worked on." Madge nodded. "Do you suppose that one of these people was the one to spot the irregularity in the accounts?"

"I don't think so," Madge replied firmly. "No one has mentioned any such thing. I think Mr. Dunphy discovered it himself. You see, he reviewed all the work done here. Often it was just a quick glance-through, but it was amazing what he could spot that way. I think he found it himself."

"Then the problem wasn't in any specific type of business."

Madge shrugged. "I've no idea."

"Did he work on a computer?"

"No. He has one in his office, but he preferred to see things on paper. He insisted that everything be printed out and filed. Before they were filed, he went through them. I know you're probably thinking that since everything is computerized, he would have been a computer whiz, but he wasn't. Both he and Elliot know how to use the computers, but neither is very good at it. They always need help. And Mr. Dunphy felt much more comfortable with material on paper. Here I am, rattling on. I'm probably boring you to tears."

"Not at all," we said in chorus.

"I just feel like talking to someone. I'm like the others, really upset, even if I have retired and don't need the job any more."

"I'm sure you must be," Douglas said. "You seem to have developed a close relationship with Owen, even if it wasn't a personal one."

"That's right. We worked well together."

I ran my hand through my hair, as if I could comb out a memory lurking at the back of my mind. "I remember us talking yesterday about security. It seems that whoever killed Owen stole the three files he was working on. Would these files still be in the computer?"

Madge frowned. "I suppose so. They must be."

"Could someone in this office go to the computer and find out which files were missing?"

Madge pulled at her lower lip and thought for a while. "I think you'd have to know what you were looking for."

"You must have a filing system."

"Oh, yes. Of course. But I don't... think... you could find out whether a file was missing unless you knew what file to look for."

"What about the paper files?"

"The same thing. They're filed alphabetically. There's no way to tell whether one was missing unless you happened to remember that there was a business with such and such a name and it should be in such and such a place."

"They're not numbered, then?"

"Not the paper files. The computer files are. But we usually just pull them up by name. There's a master list, but we seldom use it."

"What I'm getting at is whether the person who killed him and stole the printed files could have erased the computer files as well."

Madge gasped and her face lost its colour. "Oh my God!"

"If that had been done, could you tell whether it had? Would there be a number dangling out there with no file attached to it?"

"I'd like to know the answer to that one, too," said a familiar voice behind us. We turned to see Sgt. Jameson, flanked by a uniformed constable and a tall, thin, bespectacled man of about thirty in a conservative business suit. Truesdale hurried out of his office and came over.

Jameson explained, "This is Mr. Groves. He's a forensic accountant. He and Constable Marchment here are going to go over all your records until they find the missing files."

Every computer had stopped. Every head had swivelled toward the group of us. There was not a sound to be heard in the room.

SEVENTEEN

The three men from the police shouldered their way in front of us and we found ourselves being edged toward the door. As we were about to leave, Douglas remembered his original errand and turned back toward the others.

"I have to make arrangements for the memorial service." But he could not get the attention of either Madge or Truesdale.

Jameson was saying, "I'm interested in whether you can find the missing files. They probably provide the motive for Dunphy's murder, and can lead us to his killer. We want to know whether those files are still in the computer."

"Oh dear," Truesdale said, frowning. "That might be rather difficult."

"Difficult or not, I want the information. There must be a way you can check."

Groves spoke for the first time. "If I can look at your master file, I'll tell you whether there are files that have been erased. How do you get into your master file?"

"There's a code. I have it, but it isn't supposed to be used by anyone else."

"We're not going to steal your business secrets," Jameson berated him.

"If Mr. Truesdale will open the file for me, I'll take it from there," Groves stated mildly, obviously wanting to keep the people he would have to work with in a cooperative mood.

"Okay," Jameson agreed. "We'll do it that way. If Mr. Groves does find that those files have been deleted, is there any other way of tracing them?"

"Only if one of the employees remembers a particular file that isn't there," Madge chimed in. "You could ask each of them to run through their accounts and see if they notice one missing."

Groves turned toward her, recognizing someone from whom he might get some cooperation. "Just how does your system work?"

"Each employee is assigned certain accounts and always handles them. They become pretty familiar with most of them. I won't say that they will remember every single one, but someone might remember that a certain file should be there and isn't."

"Good. Let's have them do that, and I'll go over the master list and see if there are any missing spaces. That's assuming that the person who erased the file didn't also erase the reference in the master file."

"That might be hard to do. They'd have to change every reference that came after it. That's why we don't bother when we close an account."

"You don't?" Groves asked.

"No. We just leave the number there. We assign new accounts the next number in sequence."

Groves rubbed his chin. "So finding a number without a file doesn't necessarily mean anything."

"That's right."

Groves wrinkled his brow and cogitated for a minute. Then he snapped back to attention. "That brings us to the possibility that the files were not erased from the computer."

Madge groaned. "Then you'll have to go through all the files and check them against the paper ones. There are hundreds." Truesdale had said thousands, but I suspected that Madge's count was more accurate.

"Well, if we have to, we'll do it. We might get lucky and hit one right off the bat. We may only need to find one to get the information we need."

"Then what?" Truesdale asked.

"Financial affairs always leave a paper trail. Once we cross the trail, and recognize it, we can follow it. By the way, where are the paper files?"

Truesdale gestured toward a door. "They're in that room, which is kept locked, and the filing cabinets are also locked."

"Dunphy sure went in for security, didn't he?" Jameson remarked as the policemen followed Truesdale into the other room.

We managed to catch Madge's eye and she came over. Douglas broached the subject of the memorial service, saying that he would be out of town on Thursday and Friday. They tentatively set the date as the Wednesday of the following week. There was one more question I wanted to ask.

"If only Truesdale has the code to the files, how do the other employees have access to the files they work on?"

"They each have a code that opens their own group of files."

"But not anyone else's?"

"That's right."

"So if Owen had one employee's file opened on his computer at home, his killer could only erase any files that were in that employee's group."

"Oh no! Owen had a code that would open absolutely everything!"

We all groaned. I didn't envy Groves his task.

"May I make a suggestion?" Douglas ventured.

"Of course," Madge replied.

"Be as cooperative as you can. They have a job to do. They need to be able to do it. The easier you make it for them, the sooner they'll have the answers they need."

"Oh I know that." She smiled at Douglas in the fashion of a doting mother reminding a child that she knew a thing or two herself.

"Well, tell it to Mr. Truesdale."

Madge smiled and a faint chuckle escaped her lips. "I'll do that."

As we walked back to the church, Douglas commented, "There's one thing that seems obvious."

"What's that?" I asked.

"Neither Truesdale nor Madge suspects that these financial shenanigans are an inside job."

"You got that impression?"

Douglas nodded and after I'd thought about it, I said, "Yes, I think you're right. Furthermore, it seems obvious that no one in his office had any other reason to kill him."

We walked in silence for a while, then I remarked, "There's another impression I got."

"Yes?"

"That whoever did it may not have thought about having a Mr. Groves looking for his trail."

Douglas glanced toward me and smiled. "You had that feeling, too? I suspect that our Mr. Groves is going to quietly turn that whole place inside out."

I went to the airport and found two messages on my desk. Garth Hughes had set up a meeting for the following morning at his place in Pine Hill of all the flight school operators in our part of the British Columbia Interior. Could I come? He didn't waste any time, that guy.

The other message was from Clive Hawthorne. Could I fly him to Vancouver again that afternoon, returning the next day?

I handed the first message to Joyce and told her, "Tell him I'll be there."

I called Clive myself and explained that I couldn't personally fly him to Vancouver, but my regular charter pilot could. "That's okay," he responded. "Suits me fine."

"Is it just you, or is Faith going?"

"Just me this time."

We set a time and I told Terry to go home and get his overnight bag. He was planning the flight when Clive breezed in. I introduced them. Clive showed a lively interest in the flight planning process, frequently interrupting with questions that Terry answered patiently. As Terry phoned his flight plan in to the Flight

Service Station at Pine Hill, Clive frowned. After Terry had hung up, Clive asked, "Is that all the faster we're going to go? That speed you gave him seems pretty slow."

"It's in knots," Terry explained. "Nautical miles per hour. A nautical mile is 15% longer than a statute mile and almost twice as long as a kilometre, so speeds sound slower."

"Why don't the manufacturers change to kilometres? It would make their planes seem faster."

Terry laughed. "Pilots know the difference. It wouldn't matter. Besides, things have to be standard all over the world, and with the military as well. Navigation has always been done using nautical miles. At least we don't have to worry about flow, going into Vancouver East."

"Flow? What's that? I never heard of that before."

"Flow control. You've probably heard of planes being stuck in holding patterns. Well, they don't do that very much any more. Instead, they give you a time that's based on your flight-planned speed. They fit you into their traffic flow based on when they expect you to get down there into the Vancouver area. The flow time is the time you are expected to take off in order to blend into their system smoothly when you get there. If you have to do any waiting, you do it on the ground before you take off, not in the air after you get there."

"How long will we have to wait?" Clive asked anxiously.

"We won't. Don't worry. That's only if we were going into International. Then you have to take off at a precise time."

"Why can't we just take off and go? We did last time."

"We have to go IFR - that's Instrument Flight Rules. We'll have to descend through some broken cloud when we get there, and there may be some light rain. We have to get a clearance and follow it."

"Oh, I see." I was surprised that this did not seem to worry Clive, considering his reaction to our descent around and among the clouds the other day.

"Can't you just take off a little bit sooner and get a jump on them?"

Terry smiled. "No. The tower wouldn't give us a clearance to take off any sooner."

"You mean the tower here?"

"Yes."

"Why do you have to tell them?"

"I have to get my clearance from them."

"Then why don't you fudge a bit on your speed and make them think you're going to get there sooner?"

"That wouldn't work either, because we wouldn't get there sooner and we'd screw up the works."

"Y'mean there's no way at all to beat the system?"

Terry let out a long sigh. "There's no point in it. The best way to do things is to work with the system. It's designed to expedite traffic flow. If you don't get somewhere when you're supposed to, it throws the whole system off. Believe me, the easiest and quickest way is to follow the proper procedure, do your navigation accurately, and try to work with the controllers."

Clive shook his head in disbelief.

I flew my personal deHaviland Chipmunk over to Pine Hill. It's a sleek, tandem-cockpit military trainer, used for years to train Canadian and British military pilots how to fly. Mine is painted bright yellow with brown, orange and red stripes in a fan pattern on the wings and tail. It always attracted a crowd, and the other flight school operators came to give it a once-over. In spite of their fascination with that fully aerobatic trainer, it didn't seem to occur to them that students might react the same way. Garth Hughes observed the crowd the Chipmunk had drawn, however, and was impressed. The others immediately forgot, and rambled on about composites being the way to go, about the lightness of the new composite trainer, its low fuel consumption, and its overall modern design.

"But will anybody fly it?" Garth asked.

143

All eyes swivelled toward him. He repeated what he had said to me. "It looks like a goddamn toy."

They dismissed him as an old man, an over-the-hill relic of the post WWII days. If they had stopped to consider the wave of flying nostalgia that was gripping the world, they might have changed their minds. All the others voted for the new composite. Grant and I were the lone proponents of the all-metal aerobatic Czech trainer.

After the meeting broke up, Garth asked me why I didn't want to go along with the others.

"Because, if we get the Czech planes, everyone in the area will beat a path to our doors."

Garth grinned. "You wouldn't by any chance want to go into partnership with me, would you? We think alike."

My mouth dropped open in amazement. "Are you serious?"

"Never more."

The travelers returned just before noon. I listened to them on the radio as Terry made an instrument approach through a high cloud layer. After Clive had left, Terry dropped by my office.

"Y'know, for all his bluster, that guy was scared shitless when we got in the clouds."

"I know. He was that way on the last flight, and we didn't even get in the clouds, just sort of weaved around them."

"The layer is only about a thousand feet thick and the ceiling is about 4000 feet, but he didn't relax until we were on a right downwind for runway 4 and he could look down on his side and see the airport all laid out there below."

"With me, he didn't relax until he got out of the plane. He's improving," I said facetiously. "How did he act going into East Van?"

"I didn't notice. I was pretty busy. The weather was better than forecast and we didn't have to descend through cloud, but it was like rush hour on the freeway, so I wasn't paying any attention to him. I got a chance to teach him a lesson, though."

"How's that?"

"You remember how he wanted to cheat on the system by filing a faster speed or getting off the ground early or whatever? Well, some guy in a Cessna 182 did that very thing and was late getting to his approach fix. Approach Control kept bugging him to get a move on, but when they realized he wouldn't get there in time to fit into his slot, they vectored him out into the boonies and gave him a hold at some god-awful intersection I never heard of, until they could fit him in. I was walking over to the motel before he finally landed."

We had a good laugh over that. I needed a good laugh. It kept my mind off Owen's murder.

"Is this Clive guy a real good friend of yours?" Terry asked, cautiously. I could tell that Terry didn't think much of him but was wary of offending me.

"No. Why?"

"I think he's a fake."

"What makes you think that?" I asked, curiosity getting the better of me in spite of my decision that Clive was all right.

"He claims to have been in the oil business, but if he was it must have been something like driving the bus that took the guys out to the wells."

"You think so?"

"My dad is a petroleum engineer, so we've had people in our house all my life who talked to Dad about oil. I know what concerns those guys, what they talk about. I tried to ask Clive's opinion on a few things and he always changed the subject. He doesn't know beans about oil."

"He might have been exaggerating his connection in order to give a good impression. Lots of people do."

Terry snorted. "Besides, he acts as if he's rolling in dough, but I don't think he has a dime to his name."

Terry saw the blank expression on my face and laughed. "The dame pays all the bills."

"How do you mean?"

"He put the flight on her Visa card. She'd called in and authorized it and we already had her card number from the last time."

EIGHTEEN

On Thursday, Betty Forsythe phoned. "Guess what I did?" she purred in a conspiratorial tone.

"What? It sounds exciting!"

"I got Douglas a dog."

"A dog! I thought you wanted a cat."

"I do, but I know Douglas is really set on a dog. Then one of our parishioners who had heard him say so, called to tell us that their neighbour had to get rid of this lovely Cocker Spaniel, and I thought, Wouldn't it be nice to get Douglas what he really wants? So I went over there to see it and just fell in love."

"Why," I asked, suspicion evident in my voice, "did they have to get rid of it?"

"Oh, I don't know. Wait till you see him. He's a gorgeous dog."

"What does Douglas think of him? Is he happy?"

"He hasn't seen the dog yet. He's away at a clergy conference until Saturday."

"Well, if you like him and Douglas likes him, I'm happy for you both."

"Robin, come over and see him. You can tell me what you think. Come to lunch if you're not too busy."

I arrived at the rectory and rang the bell. Instantly, a great clamour arose. Could a Cocker Spaniel really bark that loud? Betty yanked open the door and yelled over the din, "Come in and meet Bonzo."

Bonzo was a good name. A muscular mass of leaping canine, covered with long, unkempt red hair, almost the colour of mine, came bounding down the steps from the living room as I entered the door, then screeched to a halt, emitted a scream of distress, wheeled and fled to the top of the stairs where it stood, shivering

147

and whimpering. I took one step toward it and it backed up against the wall, flattening itself as if it wanted to become absorbed into the wallpaper. I stopped.

"He doesn't like men. I thought," she paused, eyeing my brown corduroy slacks and green windbreaker, "that he'd be able to tell the difference."

"If he doesn't like men, how is he going to react to Douglas?" What kind of a gift is he going to be? I could have added.

"Oh, Bonzo will get used to Douglas," Betty replied airily, waving her hand as if wafting away the objection. "He got along all right with the husband in the house where I got him."

"Are you sure?"

"Oh, yes. I saw them together. I'll introduce him to Douglas, and I'm sure he will realize that Douglas is okay."

"I hope you're right," I said as we sat down on opposite sides of the room. Bonzo sidled around the room, trying to press himself into the wall, until he reached Betty's chair. He climbed into her lap, put his feet on her shoulders and turned his head to eye me with obvious suspicion.

Betty was right, though. Bonzo's curiosity finally got the better of him. He tentatively came over to sniff my shoe. I spoke soothingly and he edged closer. The first time I touched him, he jerked back as if he had gotten an electric shock, but after a few minutes he was back. Eventually, he let me pet him, then lay down at my feet. When I got up, however, he jumped to his feet and retreated under the table.

Before I left, I advised Betty, "When Douglas comes home, I think you'd better meet him in the yard and warn him."

"I did so want to surprise him, but I guess you're right." She cocked her head to one side and examined the pooch. "He's rather dirty. I'd like to give him a bath before Douglas sees him. Do you think that would be too difficult?"

"I shouldn't think so. He's a spaniel. Spaniels like water."

The week dragged by. The investigation into Owen's murder limped along, and when I ran into Madge in the supermarket, she said that Groves and Constable Marchment were still plodding through the files. They had found no gaps in the master file and no one could think of any files that should have been there but weren't. They were now painstakingly matching each electronic file with a paper one. So far, everything matched. Marchment was obviously impatient, but Groves seemed nothing other than engrossed in his job.

I awoke Saturday morning to the steady beat of rain on the roof, rain trickling down the gutters and rain being splashed by passing cars. I got up lethargically, and made my way to the airport.

Poor Lance. Another day down the drain. He could hardly contain his bitterness at the weather.

Penny called, giggling and bubbling. "What's with you?" I asked.

"I just found out something really interesting."

"Don't keep me in suspense."

"I had to go see one of our patients yesterday. She lives on Cedar Street. I usually go around by the marina and up the hill, but I was up on the Orchard Flats and I looked at my map of Exeter to see if there was some way I could get to Cedar without going clear down to the lake shore. Sure enough, Cedar turns off of London Avenue, so I thought I'd take a shortcut.

"Well, I turned off of London and went one block and found that it comes to a dead end and picks up a couple of blocks over. There's a kind of ravine there, with a dinky little creek."

"Mill Creek," I explained.

"Whatever. Anyway, I had to turn around and go back, and go all the way down to the lake. But guess what! You'll never guess what's on that one little short block of Cedar Street."

"You're right. I'll never guess."

"It's where Zane Rossiter bought his condo."

"So?"

149

"And the only buildings of any type on that side of the street are part of The Fountains!" She had named the most expensive and prestigious residences in all of Exeter.

"They're beautiful, all in tiers. They say that every apartment has a view of both the mountains and the lake. Then they have this incredible set of fountains that re-uses all its water, but looks like a terraced waterfall."

"Wow! How can he afford it?"

"That isn't all. I called him up to tell him I'd seen where he lived, and do you know what he told me?" She made the question sound as if she was suppressing a scandal.

"I wouldn't even venture a guess."

"He paid for it with his American Express card."

"What?"

"That's right. They took a look at his age and his curls and asked him discretely how much he wished to finance and where, politely but firmly telling him that it was expected that a down payment of 10% would be considered the minimum. He just casually handed them his card and said, 'Put it on this.' They wouldn't believe him, but he made them call the authorization centre, and it was authorized right off the bat."

"I wonder if it's his money or his papa's that got that kind of response."

"Who cares?"

I'd gotten a vaccination reminder card from my vet, Dr. Chris Whitney, and decided that this dreary day might be a good time to take Cloud Nine in for his annual shots. I called the clinic and made an appointment, then went home to get the cat.

He knew as soon as I opened the door that something was afoot. I don't know how he sensed it, but he was gone in a flash of white fur. I remembered hearing Chris talk on the phone to a client who was cancelling an appointment to have her cat neutered. The client had said with incredulity that the cat was always waiting on the doorstep in the morning for his breakfast, except that morning.

"You shouldn't have let him hear you make the appointment," Chris had said, only half joking.

I knew Cloud Nine's hiding places and started searching. I finally found him wedged in a crevice between the clothes dryer and the wall, so narrow that it seemed impossible for a fifteen-pound cat to get himself into it. Getting him out was like delivering a calf — all the legs got caught on anything that wasn't the least bit smooth. With the grumbling cat firmly gripped in one arm, I stood his carrier up on one end and opened the door, then dropped him into it. He hit bottom with a loud thud, emitted a venomous hiss, collected his powerful hind legs under him and shot upwards just as I slammed the door shut. It took all my strength to hold it shut and push the cat's head back far enough to get it latched.

Perhaps there were some advantages to having a dog after all. You just had to snap on a leash!

As Chris gave Cloud Nine his shot, she remarked, "Your friend, the minister's wife, came in with a new dog. She said she didn't think you approved of it."

"That's putting it mildly. What did you think?"

"He's a good, healthy dog, with nice conformation, but he's really flighty. He started to scream before I even touched him."

"I wish they'd go to a good breeder and pick out a really nice puppy. I don't think this one is going to work out."

"Maybe you should go with them the next time they look for one and veto anything that wouldn't be suitable. I don't think they know much about dogs and fall for anything that pants and looks happy when it first sees them. By the way, I like your minister and his wife. They're really nice people, and both of them have a great sense of humour. I was surprised that a minister would be like that."

"Why on earth should you be surprised?"

"I just thought they'd be sort of solemn and other-worldly, sort of staid and upright."

I sighed. "I can't think of anyone with less opportunity to shut himself — or herself — off from the affairs of this world than a priest."

"Well, I mean," Chris sounded flustered, "you'd think they would handle those problems sort of, well, reverently. I didn't expect them to make jokes about them."

"By the way, it isn't proper to call Douglas a minister. He's a priest, and he is the rector of this parish. Every baptized Christian is a minister."

"Oh? I've heard lots of people talking about their minister."

"Not Anglicans. We have priests, deacons and bishops, but we are all expected to be ministers to other people. Why don't you come with me to church some day? Now that you've met Douglas, you know that he's a down-to-earth person. He gives wonderful sermons, by the way. And we have a very good organist and choir."

"Well, I don't know…"

"Try it. You might like it."

"I'd feel awfully intimidated. I've heard people say they can't figure out the Anglican services and they're always getting lost trying to keep up with all those books you use."

"Oh, it's not that bad. I can show you how to follow the order of service. We only use one book at a time. Besides, the first time you come, you should just sit there and watch everything and let the service sort of flow over you."

"What would your — uh — priest think?"

"He would be delighted. You've met him. He won't bite you!"

She laughed. "That's more than I can say of some of my patients."

"I'm also wondering when you're going to come out and start taking flying lessons."

"Now *there's* something I'd *really* like to do!"

"What's stopping you?"

"I'll have to wait until Ted, my husband, and I can both afford it. Neither one of us would let the other go alone."

I'd decided to go to Faith's wedding after all. Clive might be an egotistical jerk, but if he made Faith happy, why should I fight it? He seemed harmless enough. I'd go kiss the bride and shake the groom by the hand and wish them well on their trip to Australia. I was choosing the clothes that I would wear, a brown checked jacket and skirt with a beige silk blouse, when the phone rang. It was Betty.

"Oh, Robin! I hope I never have to go through another morning like this." There was a hint of desperation in her voice.

"What happened?"

"I woke up early this morning and heard it raining, so I rolled over and pulled the covers up over my head and went back to sleep. Then about seven thirty, I sort of half way woke up to the sound of water splashing and Bonzo running around and yipping happily. I told myself that of course there was water; it was raining. But as the cobwebs cleared out of my brain, I realized that it shouldn't be raining *inside* the house. That got me out of bed but quick!

"I put on my robe and slippers and started downstairs, where I could hear Bonzo. He sounded like a kid with a new computer game. When he heard me, he came rushing up the stairs to meet me. I'd gotten to the landing inside the front door and could see a *flood* down there in the basement just as this great ball of soggy hair hit me right in the stomach. He was so happy, he was jumping all over me.

"Robin, you said spaniels liked water, but I never realized how true that was. He ran back down the steps, hit the water and slid down the hall until he crashed into a wall. Then he started rolling in it, came back to where I was, jumped up on me nearly knocking me down, ran up the stairs and shook himself all over the living room."

"Where did the water come from?" I asked weakly. I had a pretty good idea already, and as a member of the finance committee at the church, responsible for repairs at the rectory, I knew I wasn't going to like the answer.

"The water heater ruptured. It's a forty-gallon tank. It had all gone out on the floor, and since the water was still on, it was running all over the place. I kicked my slippers off and hiked up my robe and went wading into it. I expected it to be really hot, but it wasn't, so it must have been running for a while. Anyway, I waded into the utility room and shut off the tap. I picked up a few things that were floating around and started back upstairs to phone Nick Valutin. He's the buildings and grounds chairman, and we can't do anything to this house other than change a light bulb without getting permission. Besides, I didn't know which plumber I should call.

"Well all this time, that damn dog was cavorting around in the water like a little kid at the beach. He'd jumped up and hit me right in the middle of the back with his huge, muddy paws and knocked me down to my hands and knees in the water. So there I was at the phone, in my bare feet, dripping water, with my hair not combed, clutching my robe around me, and wouldn't you guess, when I called Nick, all I got was an answering machine. I *hate* answering machines."

"That must have been really frustrating."

"Frustrating isn't the word for it! Anyway, I left a message and tried to think who else was on the committee. I was about to call Shirley Meacham and ask. She knows everyone and everything. Then the phone rang. I thought, Oh, good. Nick's calling. He got my message. But it wasn't Nick, it was Mrs. Tregassen. George died last night."

"Oh, dear. I know he had been very sick for a long time."

"Robin, that man has been *dead* for the past two years. He was just a vegetable since he had his stroke. He could only sit up if he was strapped in his chair. He would swallow food if they put the spoon right in his mouth. Otherwise, there wasn't anyone at home any more. But the way Mrs. Tregassen carried on, you'd have thought that he was a fine, healthy specimen who had suddenly keeled over from a heart attack. She carried on something awful. I couldn't get her off the phone. I couldn't call anybody. I couldn't receive a call. I kept telling her that Douglas was away, that he'd be back by noon and I'd have him call her then. But she wasn't listening. She'd come completely unglued. She had to tell me how she met him, how he courted her, what a wonderful husband he was, how he always provided for the family, how the children loved him, what each of the children was doing now, what their plans were for coming home, what his mother had told her about George when he was a child, all the places they'd lived and all the things they'd ever done. She just never shut up."

"Frustrating," I said again. "What did you do?"

"Well, all this time, the dog was cavorting around in the water, racing up the stairs, jumping on me, shaking himself all over the place and running into the bedroom where he jumped on the bed and got the sheets all muddy."

"Oh, dear."

"I felt I had to get him out of the house, so I said to Mrs. Tregassen, 'Excuse me a minute,' put the phone down and went and threw the dog out the back door. When I picked up the phone again, she was still chattering away. She'd never missed me. I was awfully tempted to set the receiver down and walk away. Honestly, I think if I had, she'd still be talking."

By this time I was nearly convulsed with laughter, my fertile mind envisioning the situation. "I shouldn't laugh," I said, as I continued to do so. "Not when someone has died."

"Sometimes it's the only way I can handle it."

Thinking of Chris Whitney, I said, "That reminds me of something, but I'll tell you another day. What did you do?"

"I finally got off the phone. I kept telling Mrs. Tregassen I'd have Douglas call as soon as he got home, but I don't think she ever heard me. I think she just ran out of steam. All of a sudden, she said, 'I've got to go.' And *she* hung up. There I was with the phone growing out of my ear, listening to a dead line.

"By that time the dog was flinging himself at the sliding door to the patio and I was afraid he'd break it, so I let him in. Then the doorbell rang and he went into a barking frenzy. I went to answer the door and it was Nick, who had gotten my message and decided to come over when he couldn't get through on the phone. Well, Bonzo took one look at him and went into hysterics, and I must not have been much better. There I was in my dripping robe and bare feet, with my hair standing on end, gabbling about Mrs. Tregassen. Nick didn't know whether to come in or not. Then the plumber drove up. I shut Bonzo in the bathroom, which he proceeded to totally wreck, and the men went downstairs and went to work. I'll say one thing for that plumber. He got the work done fast. He probably didn't want to spend one minute longer than he had to in that loony bin."

She stopped for breath for a moment, then went on with her narrative. "They vacuumed up the water with a big Shop Vac and got the new tank installed. Everything was sopping wet. All the carpets smelled mouldy. The plumber got out a big fan and set it up. Nick had brought one, knowing what to expect. We have a big box fan, and the guys decided to set that up also, but they couldn't plug it in where they had the others, so they asked for an extension cord. I'll swear that two weeks ago I was trying to get something out of the closet and it kept getting tangled in at least three extension cords that were stored there, but do you think there was one there today?"

"Of course not!" I exclaimed, well aware of the capricious behaviour of inanimate objects.

"So I had to run down to the corner store to get an extension cord. I'd thrown on some old clothes and run a comb through my hair. I left my wet robe hanging over the bathtub, dripping. The wet slippers were still on the landing inside the door. The place was a mess, but I hadn't had time to clean it. I thought about throwing the dog back outside, but he'd worn himself out by then and was sacked out on the couch (which will never be the same), dead to the world, so I just left him.

"I didn't expect Douglas back until noon, and I was only going to be away for a few minutes, so I didn't think I needed to leave a note on the door for him. The guys had gone by then. I locked up and hot-footed it down to the store.

"Well, wouldn't you know! Douglas got home while I was away!"

"Oh, oh!"

"He says he was only mildly surprised by trickles of water where they shouldn't have been, but put it down to the rain. He opened the door with his key, stepped in, said, 'Hi, honey,' and started to take off his rubbers when he heard padding footsteps and looked up. He says he doesn't know who was more surprised, the dog or himself. They stared at each other for a moment, then Bonzo let out one of his banshee screams. You've heard him. You know what I mean."

"I know!"

"I guess he tried to run downstairs, but found his way blocked by this great, whirring fan, turned around, saw Douglas blocking his way and went totally berserk. Here Douglas had walked peacefully into his own home, expecting a warm welcome, and he was met by a totally freaked-out dog, the whirring of fans, the stench of mouldy carpets, and total destruction everywhere he went. Fortunately I got back and got the dog outside. Douglas, quite naturally, wanted to know what this schizophrenic dog was doing in the rectory. I tried to explain that I'd gotten it as a present for him. He said something like, what had he done to deserve a present like that?

"Well, the conclusion of the story is that I took the dog back where I got him and left him there before anybody could object. Douglas muttered something about going to the church to work on his sermon for tomorrow, but if he's there, he's not answering the phone. One more day in the life of a rector's wife!"

"What did Mrs. Tregassen do when she got Douglas on the phone?"

Betty gasped. "Oh, dear! I forgot to tell him!"

NINETEEN

There were about fifty people at Faith's wedding, mainly the older ladies of the parish. I wondered whether their attendance was merely because of friendship with Faith, or whether they were dreaming of the possibility of an elderly knight in shining armour coming to sweep them away, as had happened to Faith.

Betty was playing the organ, as she sometimes did at weddings and funerals. She was quite a good organist, but John Vieth could not be budged out of his seat on the organ bench for regular services. Before the Forsythes had come, John frequently complained about "lumbago" and often did not turn up for services. At these times, an elderly lady, who was a terrible performer, was pressed into service. Like a hockey goalie or football quarterback whose team has acquired a competent backup, John responded to the competition. He was not about to be upstaged by Betty.

Betty had pulled herself together after her morning ordeal and one could not tell that anything was wrong. She played the Mendlesohn wedding march, Faith having decided that the Wagner one was inappropriate.

Faith wore a simple pale lavender dress of some exquisite fabric that needed no ruffles or frills to look stunning. Her matron of honour, Mae Willoughby, another white-haired elderly lady, wore a simple light blue dress. Faith's earrings and single strand necklace were obviously of real pearls, and were vastly superior to my fake ones. Clive and Don Urquhart, his best man, wore excellently tailored tuxedos with white jackets. From the rear, you couldn't tell that they both wore wigs. I wondered idly if Clive was as bald as Don. The rings sparkled with diamonds. I tried to estimate how much of a new airplane I could have bought with the jewellery Faith and Clive were displaying.

Following the ceremony, there was a catered reception in the church hall. It was not elaborate, even though it was elegant, and it soon broke up so that the bride and groom could change and have plenty of time to catch their plane. The weather had cleared, now showing only patchy cloud. It would be another nice day for Faith's flight to Vancouver. After that, one 747 flight was very much like another and it didn't much matter what the weather was like over the vast expanse of the Pacific Ocean.

(I learned later that Lance Brock had been able to fly also. He was still putting all his heart and soul into his lessons.)

Betty met me outside the hall, a worried expression on her face. "Douglas has been locked in that office all day. He finally opened the door for me and we had a short chat. I apologized and told him I'd taken the dog back, but he seemed pre-occupied. And I think he's been smoking again. It's been nearly two years now, and I was hoping he'd quit for good, but I could smell cigarette smoke in the room."

After Betty had left, I ran into Don Urquhart, still in his white jacket, but with his black bow tie hanging askew, his collar unbuttoned, a cigarette dangling from the corner of his mouth. He was frowning.

"What's bothering you?" I asked. "Everyone seems to be in a bad mood today. Only the bride and groom were smiling."

Don took a long drag on his smoke, exhaled through his nose, took the cigarette out of his mouth and eyed it as if wondering what it was doing in his hand. "Oh, I'm happy for them. But not for the church."

"Why not?"

"You know I'm the Planned Giving officer for the parish?"

"Yes."

"It took me several months of working on Faith, but I finally secured an arrangement with her where the church would benefit from a substantial legacy. There are ways where we can borrow on our future expectations. You know all about it."

I nodded. In my capacity as a finance committee member, I'd gone to the sessions where this had been explained, even though I didn't have the kind of assets Don was interested in. My assets had wings on them.

"Faith came up to me before the service and said she had something to tell me that couldn't wait until she got back from Australia. She had made a new will, and except for special bequests, Clive would get most of her estate."

"That's to be expected."

"Yeah, I know. But that rich bastard doesn't need it. The church does."

He smoked for a moment in silence, dropped the butt on the sidewalk, ground it out with the sole of his spit-polished black shoe, then went on, "She told me in that very arch and condescending way that some rich people have, that of course there would be a small bequest for the church. When she dies, that is, which will probably be another twenty years. I'd sort of planned on having that money now. There are things we could do with it."

"There always are in a church."

"We'll probably get some from Owen's estate, but he was one of the few people in the parish who tithed, so we'll lose out there also." He was referring to the biblically recognized standard for giving to the church: to tithe is to give 10% of your income.

"Owen never impressed me as having a lot of money, but I guess he did," I mused.

"Yeah. He was happy with the simple life. That duplex of his was fine and dandy with him. He didn't want anything more. That's what broke up his marriage."

"I didn't know he'd been married."

"He was. Years ago. He had a well-paying job in a big firm and his wife thought they should be living higher on the hog. He was happy with the small house they'd bought and didn't much care about social life. So she ditched him and ran off with some junior exec with big ideas."

"Sounds as if he was better off without her."

"Probably."

"Does Douglas know about Faith's new will?"

"Yeah. I dropped into the office on my way over to the reception. He'd been working in his office and didn't want anyone to know he was there, but he'd come out for something. We went into his office and shut the door. I told him about it, then went to the reception."

I almost shouted for joy, but thought it would have offended Don, who took money so seriously. It hadn't been Douglas smoking in there. It had been Don! I was also amused at Don's characterization of Clive as a rich bastard. That put Don squarely in the same category.

That evening, I again met Madge in the supermarket and she also was frowning. No one is happy these days, I thought. I asked her in a non-committal way how things were going at the office. I didn't want to stick my nose into other people's business if I wasn't wanted, but she had no qualms about unburdening herself to me.

"We couldn't get any work done. It's income tax time. We're extremely busy as it is. I didn't realize how disruptive this police investigation was going to be."

"What can you do about it? I don't suppose you can tell the police to shove off."

"In a way we did. They aren't unreasonable. I offered to come in evenings and weekends to help them and let the others do their regular work during the day. Elliot didn't like it very much, because its not something we usually do and he's very hidebound, but he eventually agreed. Groves consulted Sgt. Jameson, who I don't think was too keen either, but I told him that if we didn't get our clients' tax returns in on time, we'd be liable to pay everyone's huge fines and we'd lose all our clients. They're edgy anyway. We've already lost a few. So the sergeant agreed and said there were some other things Groves could be doing. Groves said he had some work to do in Vancouver for a couple of days and also was going to check with other accountants to see whether any of them have noticed something odd in any of their accounts."

"That explains why one of our parishioners, who is an accountant, was complaining about the police coming to him with impossible questions at his busiest time of year. He said there was something odd in half the accounts he handled."

That brought a laugh to Madge's previously serious face. "There are in ours too, but that's not quite what they're looking for."

"How is this new arrangement working out?"

"Quite well actually. It is calm and quiet in there. It's surprising how much we can get done when there are no distractions. Actually, I like that Mr. Groves. He really knows his stuff. He knows all the dodges people use. He's not a policeman, you know. He has his own business and contracts out to the police when they need him."

"Maybe he would be interested in taking over Owen's business."

"I doubt it. He has a successful one, himself. And he has something he'd never get at our place. Well, that's not quite true because he's getting it now, but he wouldn't have a steady diet of it."

"I suppose forensic accounting, or forensic anything would be an adventure."

"Yes. That's the way he sees it. He looks very mild and bookish, but when he gets on the trail of something, he gets very intense. He makes it seem exciting."

"Maybe he'll steal you away and you'll go work for him."

"Not on your life! I'm retired, remember. I want to put my feet up and rest." She prepared to wheel her cart on down the aisle.

"Well, I don't imagine it will be long," I remarked in parting.

On Tuesday I went to morning prayer. Douglas was his normal self, the dog incident over and done with. Betty told me that the new water heater had gotten a good inauguration, as she had to wash nearly everything in the house.

After the prayers, Douglas asked me to come into the office. As he entered the numbers in the vestry book, he asked me, "How would you like to lead Compline Sunday night?"

I pointed a finger at my chest. *"Me?"*

"Yes. You." He glanced at my face and started to laugh. "Don't be so dumbfounded. If Owen could do it, you can."

My attitude hardened immediately. "If you put it that way, I certainly can."

"Good. I'll go over it with you, but you probably know it pretty well by now anyway. Betty and I are going to Georgetown to help Bishop Michael celebrate his twenty-fifth wedding anniversary. We don't know Geraldine very well. By the time he met her, I was an old married man with a couple of babies. Michael, Betty and I were quite close friends at university, though, and we like Gerry.

"That sounds like fun. I never made it to my second anniversary."

Douglas didn't say anything, but waited for me to go on. I didn't, so he changed the subject. "Let's get a *Book of Common Prayer* and go over the service. It starts on page 722."

He leafed through the book until he had found the place and we went through the service section by section. He picked up another book and murmured, "Let's see what the scripture readings are going to be. It's the fourth Sunday of Easter."

I had never realized until I joined the church that Easter is not just a day, it's a season. It lasts until the day of Pentecost, which would be in late May, fifty days altogether, the time of Jesus' post-resurrection appearances to His disciples until His ascension into heaven. Douglas found the reference and wrote down the appropriate Bible passages.

"Now, when you get over here to the confession and absolution, remember that only a priest, or a bishop, can pronounce the absolution."

"So I skip that?"

"What you can do is to read it as a prayer. Where it says, 'May the Almighty and merciful Lord grant unto you pardon and remission of all your sins,' etc., you can say '...grant unto *us* pardon...' etc."

"I see."

"You can give a homily if you want. It would come just before the Creed."

"I don't think I could do that!" My response was emphatic.

"You don't have to. But you might decide you want to. Keep it short; about five minutes."

"If *I* did one, it would be *very* short."

"Don't underestimate yourself, Robin."

As I left the church, it occurred to me that Douglas was doing to me exactly what I do to beginning students: give them tasks that they think exceed their ability in order to push them toward greater levels of achievement; of confidence as well, when they realize they can actually accomplish what has been asked of them. Well, it was okay for him to ask me to lead Compline, where I could read everything out of a book. But I couldn't possibly give a sermon, even a brief one called a homily. That was out of the question.

Was it? Of course I could! I knew exactly what the subject of my homily would be. Again, God must have reached out and touched my mind. It was all there. The sermon was all laid out before me. The realization was appalling. I, Robin Carruthers, knew the answer to something others agonize over all their lives! I hadn't figured it out on my own. The answer had been given to me, just at the time I needed it!

Now, I asked myself, since I've figured out one of the great mysteries of the Christian faith, why can't I do the same thing with the mystery of Owen's death?

TWENTY

That afternoon, Zane Rossiter flew with me on his first progress check. If you'll pardon the pun, he passed it with flying colours. He also exhibited a great deal of self-confidence. Most applicants are terrified of failing, and shun any hint of celebration until after it is over. Not so Zane. As soon as the analysis of his performance (I hate the term "debriefing") was finished, he opened the back of his van and produced a tub of ice in which rested two bottles of champagne. It is amazing how many people the sound of a popping cork will attract. You'd think he had passed his flight test, the way he was celebrating. But I realized he merely liked an excuse for a party, and enjoyed sharing with others.

Lance Brock had dug up some money, bought a chunk of block time, and was flying every evening that the weather would allow. He was heading out for his flight when the champagne began to flow. He stopped, irresolute. Celebrate or fly? He couldn't do both. The pain of his dilemma showed clearly on his long, thin face. Zane noticed him, discovered the problem, and said, "Go fly Lance. I'll keep some on ice for you when you get back."

"Thanks," Lance mumbled. "And congrats." He sounded miserable.

As the party broke up, Zane took me aside. "I'm having an open house at my new condo on Friday night. I'd like you to come."

"I'd love to. What time is it?"

"Oh, sevenish. Nothing formal. Don't dress up. And don't bring a gift. It's not that kind of affair. There'll be a number of my friends. Some are even coming up from Vancouver. And I've invited everyone else who lives in the place. I guess Penny's told you I bought a condo in The Fountains."

"She did, indeed. I'm impressed."

165

Zane chuckled. "I think it knocked her for a loop. She'll be there and sort of act as hostess, so the reason I'm asking you in private like this is that I'm not inviting anyone else from the school and I don't want Jan to know. I don't want to have to explain Jan and Penny to each other." He glanced surreptitiously around as if expecting spies in trench coats to pop up from behind the parked planes.

I frowned. "How many other girls do you have on your string?"

"None. Honest! I like Jan, and I like to take her out to lunch when we fly together, but Penny's my serious girlfriend."

"Okay. I won't tell anyone here, but you be careful. Both those girls are special to me and I don't want them hurt."

"Else the wrath of God might fall on my head." Zane grinned and elfishly cocked his blond curls to one side.

"Something like that," I muttered darkly.

The memorial service for Owen was held on Wednesday afternoon at three o'clock. Many parishioners were there, and the entire staff of his business came as a group, walking the two blocks from the office.

St. Matthew's was one of the few churches in the downtown area. Most of the city's houses of worship, being of more recent construction, were located in the outlying residential areas. St. Matthew's was Exeter's oldest church, originally a frame building located a few blocks down the street. The congregation had moved into the "new" edifice, an impressive stone structure in a park-like setting, in the nineteen twenties, when the entire city had a population of less than ten thousand. Of those people, most were Anglicans. The Roman Catholic Church, the second to set up shop in Exeter, was still small. Now it is the largest denomination, and occupies a huge complex, constructed in the sixties.

Exeter's churches exhibit a hodgepodge of architectural styles, most of the larger ones reminding me of warehouses with stained glass windows. The smaller denominations usually occupy second-hand buildings originally designed for something else. One of the new churches, having a central core and sprawling wings, is frequently mistaken for a motel. When I first came to Exeter, I thought that St. Matthew's was the only one in town that actually looked like a church, and correctly guessed that it was Anglican. I have met members of other congregations who consider St. Matthew's to be an old pile of stones and much prefer the modernistic designs of their own places of worship. The current fad is to discount the importance of the building altogether. Try telling that to a member of St. Matthew's parish!

I had never been to a memorial service in an Anglican church and came wondering what sort of a creature it might be. It was, it turned out, merely a funeral without the body.

John Vieth, at the organ was playing Bach, quietly and unobtrusively, as I entered the church. Parishioners were scattered about in the middle of the nave. No one likes to sit in the front pews for fear of seeming pretentious. Owen's employees sat in a group near the back, but Harry Meacham, seeing them do so, went to them and invited them to come to the front. I sat opposite the group and surreptitiously watched them. Some were nervous, unsure of what was expected of them. Others slipped to their knees and prayed. A few kept stony countenances, showing no emotion.

I noted with surprise that the liturgical colour white, the colour of celebration, as well as purity, was in use. Later, when I asked, I was told that black for funerals is out. No longer do we mourn the dead; instead we celebrate. We celebrate the person's life, and we rejoice in their passage into God's new kingdom.

Douglas entered, clad in a white alb and wide, black prayer scarf. After brief opening remarks (eulogies are not a part of the Anglican service), he began the funeral liturgy.

> *"I am the resurrection and I am Life, says the Lord.*
> *Whoever has faith in me shall have life, even though he die.*
> *And everyone who has life, and is committed to me in faith,*
> *shall not die forever."*

There were hymns, psalms and scripture readings, and prayers led by Shirley Meacham. One reading was done by a member of Owen's staff, one of those who had knelt to pray, the others by members of our own congregation. The hymns were of the old faithful variety. Elspeth Dodderington, our choir director, who sat beside me, told me they were ones Owen always asked her to program for the services. When we came to the anthem with the phrases, "You only are immortal, the creator and maker of all; and we are mortal, formed of the earth, and to earth shall we return," the very pregnant receptionist, Kari, covered her face with her hands and sobbed quietly. Madge, sitting beside her, put her arm around Kari's shoulder. Kari straightened up and wiped away her tears as Douglas said, "Into your hands, O merciful Saviour, we commend your servant, Owen. Acknowledge, we pray, a sheep of your own fold, a lamb of your own flock, a sinner of your own redeeming. Receive him into the arms of your mercy, into the blessed rest of everlasting peace, and into the glorious company of the saints in light."

After the service, I waited for Douglas in the office. I had a confession to make. But before I could bring myself to speak, he asked, making conversation "Have you thought up a subject for your homily?"

"Yes, I have."

"Oh, good. What is it, might I ask?"

"You might ask, but I'm not sure I'll tell you."

"I may have to go and find out."

"If you go, you might as well lead Compline and I'll be out of my sermonizing job anyway."

He laughed at that. "Not necessarily. As a matter of fact, we have decided not to leave for Georgetown until Monday morning."

"Oh!" I must have sounded deflated.

Douglas stopped, turned toward me and scrutinized my face. "I knew you'd be keen on leading Compline once you thought about it. Don't worry. You're still going to do it. I'm going to take the night off!"

"Then I don't suppose you'll come."

"I thought I would. Shirley tells me that you have asked all your bible study group to come so you won't be talking to yourself." He grinned and I nodded acknowledgment.

"I've asked some others also."

"I'm sure you'll have a good turnout. Betty thought that I probably shouldn't go. She said it might make you nervous and that I should leave you in peace."

"I'd like you to come."

"Would you?"

"Yes. Really. I — I have something to say that I'd like you to hear." Why did I get tongue-tied and start to stammer whenever I tried to talk to Douglas about anything spiritual?

"We'll come then, if you really want us to."

I nodded, then added, "I'm trying to get at least one non-member, actually, a non-believer, to come. I'm working on Chris Whitney."

"The vet?" Douglas asked with a smile as he slipped out of his alb.

"Yes. It's important to me to see if I can put my point across to a non-believer."

"But you're not going to tell me what it is?" he teased.

"No. Just don't expect one of your polished sermons. It will be pretty amateurish."

He hung up his alb and donned his jacket. "Don't worry about that. I've had lots of practice. I daresay if you let me try to fly your plane, we'd end up in a nose-dive."

"No we wouldn't," I laughed. "I wouldn't let you."

"Robin, you lack faith!"

"Speaking of faith, that's why I'd like you there. I think I've just passed a milestone. That's why I'd like Chris Whitney to come also. I think maybe now I can explain my faith a lot better. I'd like to be able to explain it to a person of my type, my background. I'd

169

like to help someone else find a way to — well, to believe. It's frightening, you know."

"What are you frightened of? You've come a long way, Robin."

"Not me! Others. People like Chris. It's frightening for them."

"Would you like to explain? Sit down." He motioned me to a chair and I collapsed into it.

How to explain. I ran my fingers through my short, red hair. "I used to wonder at the statement, referring to soldiers, that there are no atheists in a foxhole. I thought that would be the last place you would find anyone who believed in God. After all, what worse place could you find yourself in? Kill someone or be killed. Blow up houses and bridges, or be blown up yourself. Surely you must think that God had forsaken you, if you thought about God at all." Once I had gotten started, the words poured out.

"But now I think I understand. If you are in a hopeless situation, you'll clutch at anything that might give you hope, even something you had never previously believed in. Let's say your ship has been sunk and you find yourself alone on a tiny life raft in the North Atlantic in the midst of a winter gale. You know that the next huge wave is going to swamp your raft, throwing you into the frigid sea, where your survival time is measured in minutes and there isn't another ship or plane that can arrive on the scene for hours. All you can hope for is a miracle, that God will somehow lift you out of the sea and transport you to dry land.

"If you're realistic, you will remember that God doesn't do that sort of thing. God may not save you from a premature death, but you might hope that if God will not rescue your body from sure disaster, He may at least rescue your soul, and grant you admission to His heavenly kingdom. Without God, you have no hope. So you have no reason not to embrace Him."

Douglas waited for me to go on.

"But take people like myself, and Chris, and others of our generation; educated, successful business and professional people.

We're in the upper middle class income bracket, we own our homes, we have nice cars, we give our kids computers for Christmas, and on weekends we invite the neighbours over for a barbecue in the back yard. Life is all right. If we occasionally question whether life is as good as it should be, we think that if we work a little harder, get the jump on the competition, make ourselves better known, we'll solve the problem. We're materialistic, success-oriented and practical-minded. So if you come at us with some tale about how our life can be much more rewarding if we surrender ourselves to God, we're going to ask for a high-altitude enroute chart with the airways clearly marked, and a clearance from Air Traffic Control."

Douglas allowed himself a throaty chuckle.

"To admit that there is something we need that we can't get by our own hard work is threatening. To accept God is to give up our comfortable lifestyle in the hopes that we will get in exchange something infinitely more rewarding. But to be asked to accept a new lifestyle on faith alone is downright frightening! The things we fear most are ridicule and rejection. And what if it doesn't work after all? We really fear failure. We have to have some very powerful incentive to push us over the line. The shipwrecked sailor has that incentive. We don't."

"*You* must have had."

"Yes. I've been trying to figure out what it was. I feel I was pushed, no that's too strong — nudged would be more like it — by God. There was also an element of invitation. He finally got through to me."

"That is the way God works. If you have studied the Gospel carefully, you will remember that Jesus, who is God in human flesh, constantly invited others to join Him. There was never any coercion, no threats of dire consequences if they didn't, only an open invitation."

"I still can't figure out why I accepted it. When I did come to a realization that I could believe in God, it took me a long time to come to you and talk to you about it."

"I remember," he said leaning back comfortably in his chair.

"I was terrified that you would reject my unorthodox beliefs and tell me to get lost."

"Your ideas were not as unorthodox as you may think."

"I know that now. I can still recall the incredible joy when I realized that you had always accepted me in spite of my craven doubts. I'd like to be able to tell that to other people, but I can't find the words. I think people have to be receptive themselves in order to understand you when you try to talk about God's grace. It's difficult to put into words."

"You think you might be able to Sunday night, however?"

"Not that. Something else. I've found a way to talk to my kind of people in terms they can understand."

Douglas leaned back in his chair and thought for a moment, then he said, "There is another way of understanding the soldier in his foxhole or the person in the life raft." He swivelled his chair around toward me. "Remember the Beatitudes?"

I nodded.

"Think about the very first one. 'Blessed are the poor in spirit, for theirs is the kingdom of heaven.' In other words, we might say, 'Blessed are the downtrodden, the hopeless and the helpless.' The people at the bottom of the ladder, the ones who have nowhere to go, the ones in mortal danger. These are the people who are most open to God, the ones who have the most room to be filled with the Holy Spirit. We find this unnerving. We don't think we will ever be in that position. But sometime in our lives we will. You yourself came into the church out of a desire to thank God for His bounty, for his gifts to you. But there will be a time when you will find yourself in a position like that of your drowning sailor."

Douglas studied my face, which must have shown the scepticism behind my frown. He went on, "It may be a serious illness; cancer or a stroke. Or it may be something that happens to someone near and dear to you. It may even be a crash in the wilderness, but knowing your skill, I doubt that."

"I don't. I know it can happen. The knowledge that it can happen helps keep me sharp. It's the pilots who think they can handle anything that are in the greatest danger."

"Whatever it is, there will be something in your life that will be beyond your control, when you will be in most need of God's help and most open to receiving it."

"When I become a sheep," I said, accompanying the remark with a little laugh.

"I beg your pardon?"

"A sheep. I was thinking about the part of the memorial service that goes, 'A sheep of your own fold, a lamb of your own flock, a sinner of your own redeeming.' I was wondering whether I'd really like someone saying things like that about me after I die. A few years ago, I'd have been offended about being called a sinner, but I've gotten past that. I know I'm a sinner, but I also know that if I truly repent, redemption is assured. It was the sheep that bothered me."

"Why?"

"I grew up around sheep and sheepherders. Sheep are incredibly stupid animals that can't survive without the help of their caretaker, whether that person is called a farmer, a sheepherder or a shepherd. You never hear of sheep escaping and going wild. A sheep that gets out of the pasture or is separated from the flock doesn't become a wild sheep. It becomes a dead sheep. To compare a person with a sheep is to say that the person can't survive without the shepherd. So the person who is poor in spirit is like the sheep, because that person needs the shepherd, in other words, God."

I watched the skin at the corners of Douglas' eyes crinkle as a grin spread over his face. "You're coming along, Robin," he said.

Before I left, I remembered the confession I had come to make; a sort of apology.

"You know, I realize now that Owen wasn't such a bad guy after all." Douglas nodded, and I went on. "His brother truly loved him, and his employees who were here today weren't merely there

173

because they got an afternoon off work. They were genuinely grieving. Anyone who is loved by both his family and his employees must be a pretty good person. Also, I realize now that Owen followed the biblical admonitions about not storing up treasure. He made a lot of money, and I understand he gave 10% to the church, but you would never peg him as wealthy by the way he lived."

"On the whole, I would say that Owen was a compassionate person with high moral values. His faults were more than offset by the good he did during his life." Douglas leaned back in his chair and steepled his fingers as he said this.

"I'm sorry I focused on the one thing that irritated me and didn't try to discover the other side of him while he was still alive."

Douglas stared out the window, thought for a few moments, then turned back toward me.

"If you look for Him, Robin, you can find the Lord in all kinds of people."

"All I know is, I'd better really get down on my knees and repent when it comes to the confession in church on Sunday."

Douglas laughed and shook a finger at me. "I want you there in church on Sunday, on your knees. I'll be watching!"

"I'll be there," I replied. "Believe me, I'll be there!"

I left the church, feeling a warm glow inside that suffused my being. If my faith in one person had been resurrected, however, I was soon to find that my faith in several others was about to take a tumble.

TWENTY-ONE

The first blow was delivered the next evening by Lance Brock. He should have returned from his solo flight at 7:30. Time dragged on; it got dark. Overdue airplanes make me jumpy, like a small dog waiting for someone to open the door and let it out, so I was watching each plane that came in. I could see the landing light of a plane on final approach, but after watching it briefly, I decided it wasn't Lance in a Cessna 150; it was approaching at too high a rate of speed. Still, I watched it land, and as the dark silhouette of the plane passed in front of our ramp, I could see that it was a 150 after all. Not Lance, though, I told myself. He had been flying quite well lately, and this pilot was making his approach with no flaps, hot and high. The plane touched down at midfield and took the remainder of the runway for its rollout.

Soon, however, a shape loomed up on the taxiway; the 150, being taxied much too fast. While the plane was still rolling, the lights suddenly went out, which meant that the pilot had cut the master switch without turning off the individual lights. The 150 lurched to a halt, Lance Brock flung open the door. Hastily he pushed the 150 onto its tiedown spot, somewhat askew, and didn't bother to secure it. Grabbing his flight case and the clipboard that belonged with the plane, he hurried toward the office. I stepped out the door. He tried to sidle around me, scurrying sideways like a crab that has sensed danger. I blocked his way.

"Lance!"

He came to a halt and faced me, hesitantly. I stood there, arms folded, brow furrowed. He tried to pull himself up to his full height, which was still an inch shorter than mine. Some men can be thoroughly intimidated by women who are taller than they. Lance was one of them. He resented it and resorted to bluster.

"Let me past," he demanded, his tone acknowledging that he knew I wouldn't.

"Not until you park that plane correctly."

"You can have your fuckin' plane," he muttered truculently.

"You've broken a couple of cardinal rules. While the plane is still in motion, you have to give your undivided attention to where you are going. You were taxiing much too fast, and while you were still moving, you cut the master switch."

"So what?"

"You know perfectly well that at night, the lights are not to be turned off until the engine has been shut down and the propeller has stopped. Otherwise it is a hazard to anyone in the vicinity who can't see the prop. You are to stop the airplane, shut down all the radios, the interior lights and the landing light, then cut the engine. You don't turn off the nav lights and beacon until after the engine is stopped.

"And I want to talk to you about the landing you just made."

"What's wrong with it?"

"Everything, and you know it."

"I don't necessarily have to land a plane the way you want me to."

"You do if you want to fly my planes," I retorted. I could feel my face flame as a surge of anger coursed through my body.

"Like I said, fuck your damn planes." With that, Lance deeked around me, leaving me facing a ramp full of air. I followed him into the office.

He dropped the clipboard and the key on Gayla's desk and she entered the time against the balance of the block time that remained on his account. She didn't look up or speak, and from her tense concentration on the page in the book, I realized that she was thoroughly embarrassed. I remembered the times she had given Lance little helpful hints about what was expected of him. I knew that she had been hoping, as I had, that Lance had matured and was now dedicated to being a proficient pilot.

Before Lance could get away, I asked him, "What's gotten into you? You were doing quite well and were getting nearly ready to take your proficiency check-ride."

"I don't need your fuckin' planes any more. The club got their plane back today, and it's a helluva lot cheaper to fly."

"What about your training?" All I could think of was that a couple of weeks of effort had gone down the drain like this morning's bath water. Maybe something would stick with him; after tonight's display of incompetence, I doubted it.

"I can get my commercial at the club. My buddy's got his instructor license, and he'll fly with me for nothin'."

I groaned inwardly. His "buddy" meant the young man who had given him his initial training before he came here. I was amazed that this man had been granted a flight instructor's license and determined to find out if this was true. Furthermore, he would have to work under the supervision of a more experienced instructor, and I didn't think the club had any. I watched Lance retrieve his logbook. There was no way I could deny it to him. It was his property. He walked with all the authority he could muster toward the exit, and then he blew it.

He turned back toward me and demanded in a voice that was not quite as firm as I expect he would have liked, "I want a refund on the rest of my block time."

I couldn't deny him that either, so I said to Gayla, never taking my gimlet eyes off the hesitant figure of my immediate ex-student, "Figure out what we owe him."

Gayla worked the calculator, then frowned and motioned me over. I leaned over her shoulder as she went through the figures a second time. Then I straightened up, impaled the irresolute young man with the fiercest stare I could conjure up, and told him, "You owe us $17."

"WHAT? That's a bunch of shit! I want my money."

"Lance, when you fly on block time, you get a discount. If you ask for a refund on your block time because you haven't used it all, you have to pay regular rates. At the regular rate, you have

177

spent $17 more than you've paid in. Why not leave the rest of your block time on the books and if you want to come back, it will be there? There's a year's time limit on it. You can come in any time within the next year and use it. I'd suggest that you think seriously about what you're planning to do and stick it out with us until you finish your commercial."

"Not fuckin' likely." Then with a voice filled with bluster, he added, "You're cheating me. I want my money back!"

"I'm not cheating you," I replied, unable to hide the exasperation in my voice. "You know perfectly well I'm not. I'll play fair with you. I'd like the same in exchange."

Lance's face twisted into a sneer. He answered with one word, "Shit." I couldn't tell from his tone of voice whether it was a challenge or an admission of defeat. He spun on his heel and marched out the door, flinging it shut behind him. The automatic doorstop caught it and eased it shut the last few inches, destroying the act of defiance.

I sighed wearily and went out to the 150 to park it properly, tie it down and turn off all the switches that Lance had left on. Rod O'Donnell was already on the scene. His sense of order, and his concern for the airplane, which was like a child to him, had been offended by Lance's actions, and he felt compelled to put things right.

The next evening, I examined my wardrobe, trying to decide what to wear to Zane Rossiter's party. His admonition to dress casually probably meant exactly that. Even my idea of casual clothes seemed dressy by the standards of today's youth. On the other hand, I would be hobnobbing with people who lived in homes that cost as much as I could expect to earn by the time I retired.

I discarded everything that had oil stains that wouldn't quite wash out or little triangular tears that were surreptitiously patched with iron-on tape. This left me only a few items to choose from. I selected a pair of dark green slacks and a long-sleeved silk blouse in pale green, along with a pair of brown loafers and a yellow blazer. Not the latest in women's fashion, but the best I could do.

I drove up to the forbidding gate of The Fountains and pushed the button for Zane's condo. He buzzed me through the gate and his disembodied voice gave me directions on where to park and how to find his pad. I parked my Ranger between a Ford Crown Victoria and a Mercedes, feeling decidedly self-conscious as I got out and hurried across the parking lot to the building entrance.

Zane met me at the open door of his condo, welcomed me and introduced me to several people who had already arrived. "From now on, everyone will just have to introduce themselves to everyone else. I can't possibly keep you all straight." This worked quite well. Soon the place was packed, and though I didn't remember most of the names, I sorted out two basic groups: the staid and sophisticated residents of The Fountains and the young, lively and totally disreputable-looking friends from Vancouver. Of the two groups, I liked the latter best. They were intelligent, educated, witty and not at all what they looked like. They had nicknames like Bomber, Choo Choo and Gordo. One of the girls wore bib overalls. One of the boys wore tight trousers with no pockets and carried a purse. Zane looked his usual self, his clothes a very conservative compromise between the grungy young and the sedate older guests. Still, his head of blond curls stood out in the crowd and one could always spot him.

I chose the punch (mildly alcoholic) over anything stronger. I don't go in for hard liquor, and I can't stand beer. There was wine, but the punch looked good and tasted better. Eventually I bumped into Penny. Clad in purple slacks and a mauve blouse, which showed off her curvaceous figure to good effect, a colourful scarf draped casually around her neck, she seemed to be having the time of her life. She carried a tray of snacks and I chose an assortment and held them on a small napkin.

Zane came over. We made small talk about our favourite subject, flying.

"How's Lance doing? About ready for his check-ride?" Zane asked, popping a Ritz cracker topped with cheese and a pickle into his mouth.

I told him about Lance, editing the account and trying to keep my feelings from showing in my voice. Zane frowned. "Too bad. He was doing pretty well, I thought." He shrugged. "Oh well. That's his problem." He changed the subject.

As the evening wore on, the conversation predictably drifted around to Owen's murder. Everyone had an opinion, some wildly improbable.

"What are the police doing, that's what I'd like to know," expounded an elderly gentleman with a small pot belly and neatly clipped white moustache.

"They're going through all of Owen Dunphy's files to get a line on what it was that he'd found in them. Something criminal, from what he said," I explained.

"They're taking their time. What are they looking for?"

"They don't know for sure. No one does. The killer apparently made off with some files and the police are trying to see if those files are still in the computer. It seems that there isn't any way to tell whether the files have been erased."

"Of course there is. That's silly." Zane had gravitated to our group. He seemed quite adamant about the statement he had made.

"It seems that there was a master list, but no one knows how to tell whether something had been removed. There didn't seem to be any way of checking."

"Yes there is. It's simple."

"How do you know?" I asked

"Because I set up that computer program when Owen started his business."

I nearly choked on the olive I was swallowing.

When I dared look up, Zane and Penny were in deep conversation with the elderly man, Zane explaining how the computer program worked. I was so shocked, I couldn't remember a bit of it. Was I in the presence of a murderer, one who had his arm around my best friend holding her close to him, their bodies moulding to each other to form a single unit?

Zane had arrived in Exeter at about the time Owen had made his discovery. Who could more logically have dropped by Owen's place for a visit and pumped a bullet into him when he realized that Owen was hot on his trail? This young man who seemed to have money to burn might even have heard of Owen's find from Penny. And even though he said it would be possible to spot the fact that a file had been erased, I wondered. Zane was the computer whiz. He had devised the program. It would probably be simple for him to erase those files without a trace.

Then I was brought up short by the memory that Zane had not been in Exeter on the Monday night when Owen was killed. He'd been in Vancouver packing up his computer gear.

Or had he? That would be a good excuse to get rid of Penny for the evening. Had anyone actually seen him in Vancouver?

As if reading my thoughts, someone else asked him, "Hey, if you know this guy's business, maybe you plugged him. You got an alibi?"

"Yes, I have. I went to Vancouver to move my computers. Gordo helped me pack them. That right, Gordo?"

"Sure thing," said one of the grungy youths.

"Attaboy, Gordo. Nice to have friends who'll back up your story."

"For a price, of course," Gordo shouted from the opposite side of the room. Everyone laughed. Everyone except me.

"Have the cops given you the third degree?" another guest asked of Zane.

"Oh, sure. I went down there and sorted it all out for them, told them how the program worked. That forensic accountant is a smart cookie. He had it pretty well figured anyway. We found out that nothing had been erased, so now they've got to find what it was that Owen had found. Needle in a haystack stuff."

Gordo didn't impress me as a very good witness for Zane's alibi, though I assumed that if the police had questioned him, he would have put on a much more presentable front. The police surely would have grilled him. They would have come to the same conclusion I had when they heard of Zane's involvement, and if he'd given his address as 268 Cedar Street, they would have instantly known where that was. I was certain that a very rich youth with a connection to Owen and a thorough knowledge of his computer program would have rung all sorts of bells in their minds. Either they had figured that his alibi was airtight, or they were giving him a lot of rope.

What if Penny had overheard more from Owen than she'd told us and might at some time divulge other information that would make Zane think she would be able to identify him as Owen's murderer? Might he kill her to avoid detection just as he'd gunned down Owen Dunphy?

Just when I had put to rest my concerns over Clive Hawthorne's interest in Faith LaBounty, I was now faced with a far more serious fear for my best friend. Faith was barely more than an acquaintance, but Penny meant a lot to me. Her involvement with this handsome young man might literally get her killed.

I couldn't undo the knot in my stomach for the rest of the evening.

TWENTY-TWO

Saturday dawned with a low overcast and a promise of dismal weather all day long. Not much was happening at the school. It presented a good opportunity to drop in on Chris Whitney and try to talk her into coming to Compline.

Before I could get away, Penny called. "Guess what?" Her voice held a "cat that stole the poached salmon" quality.

"What?"

"I spent the night with Zane."

The silence that rolled down the telephone line as I digested that piece of information seemed to amuse Penny no end. I heard her giggle as thoughts tumbled over each other in my mind. Penny had experienced some sort of devastating love affair at some time before I met her. She had held men at arm's length, though she could have had a date every night with a different man if she'd wanted to. That meant she didn't fall for one easily. And the one she'd finally fallen for was in all probability a cold-blooded murderer.

As the silence lengthened, she finally called an end to it. "Now Mummy, I know what you're going to say."

"I wasn't going to say anything. I'm speechless. And don't do that 'Now, Mummy' thing. That wasn't what I was thinking."

"No 'naughty, naughty' then?"

"No. You're a grown woman. If you want to sleep with him, it's none of my business." I was tempted to ask her if she enjoyed it, but wasn't sure I wanted to hear the answer.

"Actually, it was wonderful," she said, answering my unasked question. "What would you do if you could spend the night making love to a thoroughly nice man?"

"I could have recently."

"And did you?"

"No."

"No? Who was it? Oh, I shouldn't have asked that. Forgive me."

"It was Dale. I met him in Vancouver when I was on that overnight charter for Faith and Clive."

"And you didn't stay with him? Robin, whyever not?"

"Because he was Dale, that's all. Look, I'd rather not talk about him. At the risk of having you start this 'Now, Mummy' thing again, I'm going to tell you I don't think it's wise for you to get too attached to Zane."

"Oh, I'm not. By the way, he asked me to move in with him."

"*What?* Penny, you're not going to are you?"

"Of course not. I just wanted to get a rise out of you." There was laughter in her voice and I was certain that she had, as she said, found her night with Zane enjoyable. Then her tone changed. "I enjoyed the one night stand, but seriously Robin, I'm not falling for him. I'm certainly not going to live with him."

"I'm relieved to hear it, but I'd like your reason why you're not."

"It's Zane himself. He's fun to go out on a date with, and he has money, so you don't have to wonder whether he's going broke in order to impress you. But he really doesn't care for me. The only person he cares about is himself."

"Oh?"

"All these good manners, all his generosity, are merely a front. He told me himself that he learned at an early age that he could get a lot more out of people by flattery, by behaving himself, by being polite and neat and well-dressed. He does it to impress people, not because he wants to make *them* happy. He's learned that he can get the things *he* wants a lot easier by putting on a front of extravagant good manners. I don't think he gives a damn about anyone else."

I let out my breath in a long, slow exhalation and felt the tension go out of my body. At least when Zane Rossiter was arrested for murder, he wasn't going to drag Penny down with him.

I stopped at Chris Whitney's veterinary clinic on the pretext of buying some cat food, even though I still had half a bag at home. I hung around for a few minutes until she had some time between clients to stop for a chat. After some opening remarks about cats, I got down to the reason I had come.

"I've been asked to lead evening prayer at the church tomorrow night. It's a big honour. But hardly anyone comes on most Sundays, and I'm afraid I'll be talking to an empty church. I'm asking all my friends to come and support me. Would you like to?"

"Well, I don't know…"

"Don't be intimidated. Nothing is demanded of you. I'd just like a few warm bodies there."

"I haven't gone to church since I was a child. I'd feel out of place."

"There is no reason for anyone to feel out of place in our church. For simple prayer services like this, we don't even kneel. We just sit in the pews and join in the responses. They're quite simple, but you don't even need to say them if you don't want to."

"I don't want to insult you," Chris said thoughtfully, "but I've never been able to understand just what people see in Christianity. A lot of it doesn't make sense."

"In what way?"

"Well, when I was about four years old, I finally realized that Santa Claus was a fake, and it didn't take long after that to figure out that Jesus wasn't what he was cracked up to be, either. I mean, they're both characters who know whether you're good or bad and are supposed to reward the good ones and punish the bad ones."

"You have a complete misconception about Jesus," I stated hotly.

"Oh?"

"If that's what your Sunday School taught, shame on them. Jesus' message is that God loves you, no matter who you are or what you do. God's love is unconditional. His forgiveness is never withheld from anyone who truly repents, and His invitation is always open to follow Him. Furthermore, God forgets all your past sins."

Chris thought for a moment, frowning and pulling at her chin. "I just can't believe in all this supernatural stuff. Have a coffee, by the way. I'll get you a mug. The sugar and the creamer are over there."

"Thanks. I drink it black."

"You might not want it black. It's been sitting there for a while."

She was right. The coffee would have cleaned the rust off an ocean freighter.

I steered us back to the subject. "What you're saying is that if you don't understand something, then it can't be true."

"Not that exactly. What I mean is, you can't prove it. You're asked to take everything on faith."

"Can you prove everything you believe to be true?"

"I think so." Her tone was emphatic.

"If Cloud Nine had an infection, you'd prescribe an antibiotic, wouldn't you?"

Chris nodded. "Of course."

"Have you ever actually seen the antibiotic molecules chasing around after the bacteria, catching up to them and destroying them?"

"No," Chris snorted.

"Then what makes you think that if you gave him an antibiotic, it would cure his infection?"

"I've seen it work. I know he'd get better because I'd seen other cats with the same type of infection get better."

"So you trust the antibiotic."

"Sure."

"Then why can't you trust in God to work in your life? Or Jesus, who is God in human form? You may not be able to see Him work, but you can see the results."

"I've never seen any results."

"Have you looked?"

That stumped her. She thought for a moment. "Well, not really." She glanced around like a cornered animal, looking for a means of escape. She said, defensively, "What do you get out of it? It all sounds like a pretty hard life."

"God's grace."

"What's that, anyway?"

I thought for a moment. "It's hard to describe. It's sort of a feeling of being loved and cared for, and not having to worry about little things. It makes life much simpler."

"I still don't think I could ever believe in God."

"You might try opening yourself to the possibility. God found me when I did that."

Chris sighed, turned to rinse out her coffee cup. "There are other things, too."

"What?"

"Well, for one thing, Christians can't count."

That was about the last complaint I'd expected to hear, and Chris couldn't have missed the slack-jawed look of incredulity on my face. She gave me a tight little smile and waited.

"What do you mean by that?" I asked, definitely curious.

"Well, it's like this. Christians say that Jesus was resurrected three days after he was crucified. But if he was crucified on Friday afternoon and resurrected on Sunday morning, that's a day and a half. How do you get three days?"

"Oh!" I said, letting out a sigh of relief. "I can answer that."

But before I had a chance to, the outer door burst open and in rushed a frantic man carrying the limp and bleeding body of a Brittany Spaniel. "He was hit by a car. Can you save him?"

Chris sprang into action, and I plastered myself against the wall to let the man by. Chris' question and my pending answer were forgotten. I eased myself out of the clinic. I'd talk to her again another time.

***

I drove out toward the airport, even though I knew that nothing would be going on there. As I approached it, one of the new small jets broke out of the overcast and entered the downwind. I thought about Paul St. Cyr and wondered when he would be home. He was a lot better for Penny than Zane Rossiter was, and it might be good to have him around when the bottom dropped out from under.

I drove without thinking, making the proper turns, responding to traffic signals on the well-known route to the airport. While I drove, thoughts tumbled around in my mind as if they had been thrown into a revolving drum. Then they began to slot themselves into place, one after another. I slammed on the brakes and swerved over to the curb, while the driver of the car behind me leaned on his horn. I shifted into neutral, put on the emergency brake, leaned on the steering wheel and thought furiously.

Something Paul had said. Something Penny had been in doubt about. Something Chris had asked.

It all began to add up, and the answer was murder!

I took a quick look for traffic, swerved the Ranger into a U turn and made a beeline for the rectory. Douglas and Betty, seemingly startled by my mercurial arrival, said they had been leaving to look at some kittens but it could wait.

"Kittens?" I exclaimed, momentarily put off my stride. "I thought you'd decided to get a dog."

They exchanged glances, and Douglas admitted, "We decided we weren't cut out to be dog owners."

"Where are you getting these kittens?" I asked, mentally crossing my fingers.

"I was at a PLURA meeting yesterday," Douglas explained. PLURA is an acronym for the clergy of the Presbyterian, Lutheran, United, Roman Catholic and Anglican churches. "Father Joseph Quinn of the Roman Catholic Church said his organist had a litter of kittens to find homes for. Her name is Mrs. Charpentier. We called her and she has two that she wants to give away. She's keeping one. They are about six weeks old. We won't actually take one until we get back from Georgetown, but we couldn't wait to see them."

"If you have something urgent to talk to Douglas about, I'll call Mrs. Charpentier and see if we can come over later," Betty offered, then added, "Would you like to come with us?"

I accepted the offer, but steered the conversation back to the murder. Douglas listened intently for about half an hour, asking occasional questions.

"I think," he said at last, "that we had better go to the police."

Douglas called and was told that Sgt. Jameson was in and would see us. We drove to the RCMP detachment in my pickup so that Betty would have the Jeep in order to meet us at Mrs. Charpentier's. The policeman at the front desk let us in and showed us where to find Sgt. Jameson's office. As we approached it, Cpl. Marchment bustled down the corridor from the opposite direction and stuck his head in Jameson's door, exclaiming in a breathless voice, "We've got it!"

"The files?" Jameson's voice asked.

"Yeah. We finally came across the first one. We were in the Ts and about to give up hope. Theilman Engineering, it was. The others were Welco Electric and Wright Brothers Plumbing Supply, but once we had the first one, it took only minutes to find the other two."

"What was the gimmick?"

"They all had paid out on invoices from a company called Exeter Enterprises. Trouble is, there's no such company. It had a local post office box and a phone number. The invoices were for really vague things that you couldn't quite identify, like 'Management aids.' They could have been goods or they could have been services. The cheques were stamped on the back, 'Exeter

Enterprises', no name, and deposited in an account at Bank of Vancouver. The box was at the main post office, but it was closed out on the Tuesday afternoon after Easter. The phone was at one of those secretarial agencies where they'll rent you a line, a telephone and an answering machine. The messages on the machine could be picked up by dialling the number from a touch-tone phone and entering a code number, so the guy didn't ever have to come to the office. He called that Tuesday afternoon to say he wouldn't need the service any more. He'd already paid up to the middle of the month, but he didn't ask for a refund."

There was a moment's silence while Jameson digested the information. "See if you can get a description of the person who rented the box and the phone."

"The lady at the secretarial service said she can't remember him. It was eight months ago. We'll have to wait till Monday to tackle the post office, but I doubt if we'll get anything there either."

"You mean this has been going on for eight months?"

"Groves doesn't think so. He thinks it was set up months ago, then left to cool, specifically so no one would remember. He thinks this would be a hit and run kind of thing — hit a whole bunch of businesses quickly, then pull out."

"Obviously this guy didn't reckon with having any Owen Dunphys on his trail."

"Yeah. That Dunphy guy was so meticulous it was scary! What I want to know is, do we wait until the banks open on Monday, or do we drag someone from Bank of Vancouver off the golf course to go over the records?"

"I don't think we can wait. I want to come up with a name."

I stepped into Jameson's office and said to him, "If your banker doesn't recall a name right off, you might see if Clive Hawthorne means anything to him."

Marchment and Jameson both stared at me. Marchment's jaw dropped, his eyes widened. Jameson glanced at him, then swivelled his head toward me, his body tense, his lips a narrow slit. Then with a sly smile, he turned back to Marchment. "And if Clive Hawthorne doesn't ring any bells, try his real name, Melvin Kestering."

TWENTY-THREE

You could have blown me over with a faint puff of wind. I'd been gearing myself to counter the scepticism I expected when I tried to convince Jameson that Clive Hawthorne was a fake, and here Jameson knew it already and even knew Clive's real name. I had been able to convince Douglas this time, and had hoped his support would be enough to persuade the police to take me seriously. With that worry off my mind, I was sure that I could put the rest of my argument across.

"How did you know?" I started to ask, but Jameson raised his hand, palm toward me, to stop my query. "I'll ask questions first, if you don't mind."

He waved us to seats across the desk from him as he gave Constable Marchment instructions. Marchment bounded out of the room like a dog released from a chain.

"Now, what's this about Clive Hawthorne?" he asked.

"I've thought ever since I first met him that Clive was a fake, but I guess I don't have to tell you that."

"I'd like to hear what you have to say, anyway."

"At first, I just had a general impression that he wasn't quite what he said he was. The only things I could specifically put my finger on were the fact that he wore a wig and dyed his eyebrows, but I've been thinking it over lately, and there are a lot of other things, too."

"Like what?"

"His accent. I'm not convinced that it's really Australian. I think he has taken the characteristics that are popularly thought to be Australian and practiced them. But it's shallow."

"You mean there are other things about Australian speech that he lacks?"

"No. There are things about Canadian speech that he hasn't gotten rid of. I don't mean that he ends his sentences with 'eh' or pronounces words containing 'out' in a Canadian fashion. By the way, Canadians don't say 'oot' for 'out.' They say 'oat.' It's not that. It's more subtle, words we pronounce differently than people from other countries that we aren't aware of."

"What specifically?"

"Words whose last syllable start with the letter d. I heard him use two of them, pardon and student, and his pronunciation was definitely Canadian. The English, and most University-educated Canadians, pronounce those words distinctly, with all the letters intelligible and equal accents on the two syllables, or perhaps a slight accent on the first one. Americans slur the words and almost drop the d. But the average Canadian breaks the word between the syllables almost as if it were two words and puts a distinct emphasis on the d."

"Hmm. I'll have to listen for that. Anything else?"

"The word, 'student,' caught my attention for another reason. He was asked whether he played Australian Rules Football and he said he had done so during his student days. Now, I'm not sure of this, but I think an Australian would have used the word 'schoolboy.' 'Student' is an American expression, one we've borrowed from them. Aussie football brought up another thing. He says he roots for the Hawthorn team because of his name. I think it's the other way around. The reason I think so is because of the name he gave for his wife. Someone asked him what his deceased wife's name was."

"His wife isn't deceased," Jameson interjected, but seeing that I was about to start asking questions, told me to go on with my narrative.

"He seemed startled to be asked his wife's name, and didn't seem to remember it. I think he was doing some quick thinking to come up with a likely name. Let me ask you, aside from Mathilda, what woman's name would you associate with Australia?"

Jameson frowned and thought for a moment. "Alice," he said. "Because of Alice Springs. That's one of the popular tourist spots in Australia. My sister went there and did all the usual things like taking a picture of Ayres Rock right at sunset. She called the town, 'Alice,' as if it didn't have the word 'Springs' in it."

"Exactly. That's the name he came up with. I suspect that while he was practicing his Australian accent on people who didn't know him, someone asked him his name. He didn't want to give his real one, and he hadn't figured out an alias yet, but his favourite Aussie football team came to mind and he said, 'Hawthorn.' Latter, I suspect he added the silent 'e' so it wouldn't be quite as obvious to other people as it probably was to him.

"His next error also involved sports. He was asked what hockey team he rooted for. He said, 'The Canucks, of course.' However, he had supposedly just moved to BC from Edmonton. He should have said, 'The Oilers, of course, but I'll have to become a Canuck fan if I continue to live here.' Or, if he didn't think he could get away with being an Oiler fan, he would have said, 'The Canucks. I used to be an Oiler fan, but since they traded Gretzky and Messier, there's nothing to like about them any more.' I think he got caught having to make conversation on subjects he hadn't prepared himself for."

Jameson nodded, his chin in his cupped hand, his elbow resting on the desk. His thoughts were far away. Finally he brought his gaze back to my face and said crisply, "Go on."

"One of my pilots, Terry McGregor, flew him down to Vancouver the week after our first trip. He, too, thought Clive was a fake. Clive professed to have been in the oil business, but Terry's father is in the oil business, and when Terry tried to engage Clive in conversation about oil, Clive always changed the subject. Also, Terry brought to my attention another thing I had overlooked. Clive wasn't the one who paid for the two trips to Vancouver. Faith LaBounty did."

Jameson raised his eyebrows at that. His attention riveted, he bade me continue.

"Clive likes to show off a very expensive Rolex watch. But thinking back, I'm sure he didn't have it the first time I met him. I'll bet it was a gift from Faith.

"I thought from the first that he might be someone who was out to get Faith's money, but when I said he wore a wig and dyed his eyebrows and acted a little too hearty, it didn't sound like much. I also thought that Faith seemed an unlikely person for him to fall for. I can imagine her falling for his line, but his seeming to fall for her didn't ring true. I tried to disregard it for a long time, but I can't any more."

"I'm afraid I was no help," Douglas admitted.

"You reacted to him the way everyone else did. I was the oddball. And since you are used to dealing with people, and I deal more with machines, I thought you were probably right. Besides, you didn't see him that first time I did. That's when I tagged him as someone I wouldn't trust." My lowered head and husky voice laid bare my disgust with myself.

Jameson heaved a deep sigh, shifted in his chair and said, "I guess we'll have to nab him for fraud, but it'll be hard to pin on him. Even if he was using an alias, this Faith LaBounty went into it with her eyes open. I guess we could get him for bigamy, though." He chuckled. "I've never arrested anyone for bigamy. I don't see what a big deal it is, personally."

"You would if you had two wives both trying to inherit under his will, or get child support or something like that."

"Yeah, I guess so. Still, with a murder to be solved, I'm not hot to trot on some bigamy charge."

"Your murder is solved," I declared.

He stared at me intently, a frown wrinkling his forehead. "You don't mean Hawthorne, do you?"

"Yes."

"Let me remind you, Mrs. Carruthers, that your Mr. Hawthorne was in White Rock, south of Vancouver, sleeping with his wife, his real wife, I mean."

"On Monday night?"

"On Monday night, the day you flew him down there."

"I don't doubt that. But Owen wasn't murdered on Monday night. He was murdered on Sunday."

"How do you figure that?" Jameson's voice had hardened. He was willing to listen to my litany of complaints about Clive's character, but when I started to tell him he'd got the day of the murder wrong, I could tell I was in for an argument. For starters, I decided to hit him with a hard and fast fact.

"Because he was still wearing his Sunday going-to-church clothes, for one thing."

I saw a lop-sided grimace pass briefly over Jameson's face, and gathered that he was kicking himself for overlooking the obvious and not following up on it. I pressed my advantage.

"He was wearing the clothes he always wore to church. He had led Compline on Sunday night, and it looked as if he'd gone home, loosened his tie and unbuttoned the top button of his shirt while he informally entertained a guest. He wouldn't have been dressed like that on *Monday* night unless he had some meeting to go to. But remember, he was supposed to be out of town. He only stayed in order to get this material he had in shape to take to the bank, which would know who was behind this false company. He wouldn't have gone to any formal meeting on the spur of the moment, and otherwise, he wouldn't have dressed up."

"Maybe he dressed like that all the time."

"He didn't though. He hadn't even dressed up for morning prayer a few days earlier. It is much more informal."

Jameson frowned. "Anything else?"

"His office started getting calls from companies he had appointments with on Tuesday, asking where he was. He must have changed his Monday appointments, but not those on Tuesday, or the rest of the week. He was a stickler about things like that. He expected to be in Alberta on Tuesday."

Jameson digested that information without comment.

"There was no reason to wait until Tuesday. There wasn't that much information in the files for him to go over, from what I heard Constable Marchment say."

"I can think of one reason," Jameson asserted. "The banks wouldn't be open Monday. It was a holiday."

"No it wasn't. Easter Monday isn't a statutory holiday in British Columbia. Good Friday is. I know. I have to give my employees the day off or a compensatory day. Some businesses and probably government offices were shut on Easter Monday, but not the banks. I know about that, too. I went to my bank to make a deposit. Banks aren't allowed to close for more than three consecutive days and they were closed Friday."

"You are overlooking the fact that everyone agreed that on Sunday, Dunphy told everyone who would listen to him that he would go to the bank in three days."

"No. He didn't. I've had something in the back of my mind all along that was worrying me. Then today, someone asked me what seemed like a silly question, and in answering it, I realized what had been bothering me. If you recall, I told you that I'd heard it second-hand from Penny Farnham and Paul St. Cyr. I myself didn't hear it on Sunday after church, and I wasn't at Compline. But Paul St. Cyr heard it directly from Owen. Paul is a retired journalist. His training and experience were to listen carefully to what people said and to quote them exactly."

"I can't say they do it very often. Even though they shove a tape recorder almost right in your mouth, they still don't quote you accurately." Jameson let the bitterness show in his voice.

"Paul was a journalist of the 'old school' who learned his trade before tape recorders. He listened, took notes, asked questions and when he wrote his piece, he was accurate with both his facts and his quotes. Whenever there was anything regarding aviation that was newsworthy, we always tried to get Paul to cover it."

"I'm sorry. I haven't been in Exeter long enough to have met him at work."

"Take my word for it, or ask other people. He was that way. Anyway, he had heard Owen, and when he told it to me, he quoted Owen exactly, even mimicking Owen's voice. I'd be willing to bet that he didn't get more than one word wrong."

"So what did he say?"

"I've been trying to remember it exactly. I may not be as precise as Paul was, but I've got the important elements. Also remember that Penny heard Paul tell me, and she heard Owen directly, and when you asked her to verify what Harry Meacham had told you, she hesitated. I think she realized that something was wrong, but she was so shaken up by just having heard that Owen had been murdered that possibly she wasn't thinking very clearly. Then today, a friend complained to me that Christians couldn't count. I asked her what she meant and she asked how, if Jesus was crucified on Friday afternoon and resurrected on Sunday morning, we could say that it was three days later. She pointed out that it was a day and a half."

Jameson frowned in puzzlement.

I went on. "The mistake both she and Harry Meacham made is one of saying 'In three days,' rather than saying, 'On the third day.'"

"I don't get it."

"Jesus was crucified on Friday, the first day. On Saturday, the second day, He lay in the tomb. At sunrise on Sunday, the third day, He rose from the dead."

I stopped a moment to let that sink in. "What Owen said was, 'On the first day, I gather the material. On the second day, I correlate it. On the third day, I go to the bank.' We know he gathered the material on Saturday. On Sunday after church, he went home to work on it. On Monday, the third day, he intended to be at the bank when they opened at 9:30. He never got there. He was killed on Sunday night."

"You may be right about this, but it still doesn't implicate this Hawthorne character. He had an alibi for that night also. He went home with Faith LaBounty."

"He took Faith home. Remember, she said she couldn't go to Owen's because she wanted to get home and pack for her trip. Clive would merely have taken her home. She wouldn't have invited him in. If you knew both of them, you'd realize that a person like Faith wouldn't want someone like Clive looking over her shoulder while she packed her undies. That would have suited Clive just fine. I'll bet he told Owen before they left the church that he'd be over as soon as he'd taken Faith home."

Jameson sighed. "Do you have anything else?"

"I can't think of anything."

Jameson leaned back, clasped his hands across his waist and heaved a deep sigh. "Well, Mrs. Carruthers, you've given us an interesting theory to work on, but we have to prove it. In fact, what you said about the murder being committed on Sunday night brings another suspect into it."

"Who? It isn't Zane Rossiter, is it?"

Jameson speared me with his steel-grey eyes. "What do you know about Zane Rossiter?"

"He is a student at my school and dates a friend of mine."

"Miss Farnham?"

"Yes."

"What makes you think he would be a suspect?"

"He is a young man with a *lot* of money. He paid for that condo in The Fountains with his American Express card. He is a computer expert, and he designed Owen's computer program. He could have heard about Owen's claim from Penny. When we thought that the murder had been committed on Monday night, I wasn't sure that his alibi was really as good as it sounded."

"It was, though. We checked." Jameson sounded as if this had been a disappointment. "He was in Vancouver packing up his computer equipment and other things to move them to Exeter. Helping him were Gordon MacIntosh, Jr., son of Gordon MacIntosh, QC, a well-known Vancouver lawyer, and MacIntosh Junior's girlfriend, who cleaned up the apartment after the men. They then went to the manager, who inspected the apartment and refunded Rossiter's damage deposit. There's no doubt he was actually there. Also, Groves went over Rossiter's finances, and found that all his income seemed to be accounted for. He really does have fees and royalties pouring in. Groves wouldn't commit himself absolutely, but when Rossiter seemed to have an ironclad alibi, we didn't carry the investigation into his finances any further. However, if we have to consider Sunday as the day Dunphy was murdered, that neat alibi is useless. That puts him right back into the chase."

I laughed. "Well, you can forget it. He has an even better alibi for Sunday. He and Penny were out pub-crawling and movie-going until after one AM."

"How do you know?"

"Penny and I went out to dinner at the Lakeview Terrace. When we were leaving, we just happened to run into Zane. It was supposed to seem casual and fortuitous, but I expect that Zane engineered it. He invited Penny to go out with him for the rest of the evening when he found out that I had wheels and could get myself home. She did. She told me all about it the next day. You'll have to ask her, but I expect you'll find that they were together all evening, and Owen wouldn't have been entertaining anyone after one AM."

Jameson deflated, suddenly appearing tired. He smoothed down his slick hair and leaned on his desk, looking down at the papers arrayed on it.

I said, "I suppose you've investigated Garrick Dunphy's former mine manager."

"Yeah. There wasn't anything in that. The guy's wife was sentenced to house arrest, with an electronic monitor, for a year, then paroled. She got permission to move to Whitehorse, where her husband had a new job. They're still there. They were at home at the time of the murder, either Sunday or Monday."

"I hope he didn't get a job with an engineer who builds bridges."

"No. He's still in mining. Why?"

"Nothing important." I cautiously let out a sigh of relief. I figured that I'd probably like Zane's dad if I ever had a chance to meet him. Jameson was regarding me with a puzzled frown, considering, I suppose, whether to press me for details and wondering if he'd only be opening up another can of worms. He evidently decided to let the matter drop.

"Actually," I continued, "everyone who'd heard Owen talking about what he'd found had an alibi except Clive — and me. Don Urquhart and the Meachams went out to dinner. Paul St. Cyr left for England. Penny was with Zane. Faith doesn't drive and would have had to get a ride or take a taxi to go over to Owen's, which would have been totally out of character for her anyway. I went home after Penny met Zane, but I didn't go to Owen's place, in case you're interested. So, since I know that *I* didn't commit the murder, that leaves Clive."

Jameson grinned. "I wouldn't think of suspecting you, Mrs. Carruthers."

After a momentary silence, Douglas said, "We were concerned about Faith LaBounty. It appears that Clive planned to convert her assets into his name, or something of that sort. We thought he might have planned to stay with her and live off her money, but if he had a real wife stashed away, that's doubtful. He probably planned to get her money and disappear, resuming his real identity. We figured, or I should say, Robin did, that he used this scheme with the false invoices to get a little working capital so he could appear wealthy, but his real victim was Faith."

"I doubt that." The detective's forehead creased into a frown. "If we find that he is the person behind this Exeter Enterprises scheme, it's more his style. He's pulled off similar escapades before. Courting rich old ladies is something new. Assuming all you say is true, Mrs. Carruthers, I'd venture a guess that his incomplete planning was because it was a spur-of-the-moment opportunity that unexpectedly presented itself, and was outside his normal realm of operations."

We digested this information in silence, then Douglas shifted in his chair and resumed his narrative. "Then, we thought, if Clive had been found out once, had committed a murder to cover it up, and knew the police were hot on his trail and would hit upon his fraud scheme one of these days, he might get nervous and try to hurry things up."

"I know he was nervous," I added. "Both Terry McGregor and I noticed that when we were approaching to land at Exeter, he got as jumpy as a dog with fleas. When I was flying, we made a straight-in approach and he didn't calm down until we were parked on the ramp and he got out and looked around. When Terry was with him, they made a right down-wind, and Clive could have looked down from his seat on the right side of the plane and seen that there weren't any police cars waiting for him. That's when he relaxed."

Douglas continued, "We are concerned that, having committed the murder, Clive might have been convinced that he would have to get rid of Faith in a hurry. We are worried about her safety."

Jameson pushed back his chair, stretched out, ran a hand over his face and said in a sympathetic voice, "And well you might be. But you're too late. She stepped into the street in Sydney, Australia, right in front of a truck. She was killed instantly."

I heard Douglas emit a groan. As I buried my face in my hands and tried to keep from crying, I felt his arm around my shoulder. I took a deep breath and sat up.

"The police in Sydney treated it as an accident, a tourist from North America looking the wrong way before stepping into the street. Then someone they describe as 'a very reliable witness' came forward and told them that it was a set-up. A man on the other side of the street — your friend Hawthorne — waited until he saw the truck coming then called to her that it was safe to cross. They're considering it murder, but they know they'll have a hard time proving it. The woman was traveling under the name of Faith

LaBounty. I gather that they left immediately after their 'wedding', so she wouldn't have papers in her new name."

Douglas grimaced. "That's right," he said.

The man was using his real identity, Melvin Kestering. I guess he didn't want to risk using fake identity papers. It appears that he always managed to be by himself when he registered for them or had to show his passport. He registered as Melvin Kestering and wife, but the lady apparently never realized that."

"That's not hard to believe," I remarked.

"However, she did give her name to several people as Mrs. Clive Hawthorne. She signed it that way once. That's how we got into the act. The police down there contacted us to get a line on him. They gave us both names. Clive Hawthorne didn't mean anything, except as a marginal character in this murder investigation. But Kestering rang all kinds of bells. He's wanted in at least three other provinces for one fraud scheme or another. He's slick. He's hard to pin down. Well, we've got him now. He's sitting on an airliner somewhere over the Pacific, and we'll have a welcoming party for him when he arrives in Vancouver."

As we left, I could see Douglas' shoulders sagging. He looked a couple of inches shorter than usual. There was an expression of agony on his face.

I didn't envy him the task of going to see Olivia Marriott and telling her that when she'd signed Faith's marriage papers, she'd also signed her death warrant.

TWENTY-FOUR

Betty was waiting for us on the sidewalk in front of Mrs. Charpentier's home. Her uneasy look became even more anxious when she saw our faces. Douglas told her about Faith, and she buried her face in his chest, sobbing, while he enfolded her in a tight hug and laid his cheek on the top of her head. They stood that way for a couple of minutes. Off to the side, I felt a pang of regret that I had no one to hold me, no shoulder to cry on. I never had. My parents, though I had never doubted their love, were not demonstrative people. I couldn't remember being hugged. And Dale... I would prefer not to even think about Dale.

Betty finally wiped her eyes, saying, "Let's go see the kittens. Maybe that will take our minds off things for a while."

Mrs. Charpentier, a tall, dignified lady with her grey hair pulled back into a bun on the back of her head, noted our long faces and inquired whether there was anything wrong. Douglas told her briefly that we had just learned of the death of a parishioner in tragic circumstances. Jameson had asked us not to spread the news until they had arrested Kestering, lest his wife hear and take off for parts unknown. We had told Betty, and would tell Olivia Marriott, but the news would go no farther. Mrs. Charpentier expressed suitable dismay and offered condolences, then led us to the bedroom where the kittens' box was kept.

They were fast asleep. The mother cat, a smallish calico, trotted behind us and stood proudly to the side as we cooed over her babies, making exaggerated kneading motions with her front feet. A calico kitten, lying on her back, with her round belly bared to the world, heard us and opened one eye. We must have looked interesting. She tried to roll over and her contortions woke the other two kittens: a black one with a white blaze, bib and feet, and a ginger tabby. Soon all had stretched to get their immature little muscles in working order, and bounded out of the box to see what sort of entertainment we had to offer.

We went into the living room and sat down while the kittens proceeded to put on a show. They leapt about on pogo-stick legs, their exclamation-mark tails pointed skyward. Soon they were tussling with each other, growling and hissing. One would get the upper hand over another, only to have the third join the fray and tip the odds in favour of the previous underdog.

Finally they tired out. The black and white one made the rounds, sniffing our shoes, then chose Betty, climbed her trouser leg as if she had been a tree, and settled down in her lap for a snooze, purring loudly.

"We thought of calling him 'Motorboat,' because of his purr, but we decided we'd better not name them or become too attached. We're going to keep the female. Those two are males." Mrs. Charpentier indicated the drowsy black and white kitten and the ginger tabby, who had discovered an interesting corner and was investigating.

The calico kitten found a spot to flop down for a nap, but the ginger kitten was still on the go. He climbed onto the couch, scampered the length of the back, hopped down onto the arm and raced to its end, staring with myopic little eyes before launching himself into the void of space. Betty gasped as the kitten belly-flopped onto the carpet with a whoofing sound, but he got his legs under control and took off at a dead run. We could hear him as he rounded the corner into the kitchen and hit the vinyl. He sounded like a stampede in a western movie as he thundered across the kitchen, into the dining room, and back into the living room. He was puffed up to twice his normal size, his tail like a bottlebrush. Seeing us, he hopped sideways until he ran under a chair and bumped his head. He turned, spat at the audacious chair leg and stalked off. Suddenly his puffed-up fur flattened itself down like a balloon that had lost its air and he collapsed into a heap, sound asleep. We were all howling with laughter.

"Do you know which one you would like?"

I saw one of those wordless exchanges by which the Forsythes frequently communicated. A minimal raising of an eyebrow. The faint hint of a smile. Douglas turned to Mrs. Charpentier and announced, "We'll take both of them."

I hadn't even given the murders a thought since I'd walked into the house.

Before church the next morning, Betty told me, "We decided to call the kittens Shadrach and Meshach. We told Mrs. Charpentier and she said, in that case, she'd call the other one Abednego, but since that is a man's name, she'd shorten it to Abby. I can't wait to take them home."

After church, I went with Betty to the office and found Sgt. Jameson waiting there. Betty told him that Douglas would be along after he had greeted all the parishioners as they left the church. When Douglas joined us, Jameson relayed the information that Melvin Kestering, alias Clive Hawthorne, had been arrested when he had arrived in Vancouver. His wife was waiting for him. They had tailed the couple to their car, where Kestering had removed his wig and his false eyebrows (this got an exclamation out of me) and had also pulled off some small strips of tape that tightened the sagging flesh of his face and gave him an entirely different appearance.

"He's a master at disguise," Jameson told us. "I'll bet that when we show the real Kestering to the manager of the bank, he'll recognize him. A picture of Hawthorne, actually his wedding picture in the paper, didn't get even a flicker of recognition from him."

"Was Mrs. Kestering involved in the plot?" Douglas asked.

"Mrs. Kestering, when she heard about Faith LaBounty's death, sang like a canary. She admitted to taking part in the fraud schemes, but denies any knowledge of anything violent. I guess Kestering had been able to convince her that he didn't have anything to do with Dunphy's death, even though she was suspicious and grilled him about it. He told her that Dunphy was disliked by a lot of people and had lots of enemies. Is there anything to it?"

"He annoyed a number of people, including me," I volunteered. "But it wasn't the kind of thing you'd murder him for. Besides, he was basically a good person. He had a lot of friends. People respected him, and his office staff seemed to think he was a good employer."

"Well, anyway, he put it over on his wife. They didn't have time to discuss anything before we arrested him. I guess he'd just called home from Australia, said he had ditched the lady, but didn't say anything about her being dead. Mrs. Kestering thought it was part of the normal scheme. She called him all kinds of names, which I won't repeat, when she was told about the murders. She's completely disowned him. She may just be trying to save her own skin, or she may be telling the truth. They've pulled a number of schemes before, but there's never been any violence involved."

"That fits. He seemed awfully nervous. I wouldn't have thought a hardened killer would have. I wonder why he didn't just pull up stakes and disappear when he knew he'd been found out, or at least was on the verge of being."

"Greed, I expect." Jameson, who had been perched on the edge of a desk, got up and moved toward the door. "The LaBounty deal was too good to let go."

"So you've got everything wrapped up?" I asked.

"Not quite. But we'll get there."

"The Mounties always get their man."

Jameson grinned at me, but said nothing. He turned to Douglas. "Mrs. LaBounty's ashes are being shipped back from Australia to this church. She didn't seem to have any relatives to claim them."

Douglas nodded. "That's fine. We will give them a proper burial."

The tight feeling in my gut reminded me of my vexation over having failed to put all the clues together in time to save Faith's life. Visions of Clive's cheery face kept flashing through my mind. I couldn't imagine him as a murderer. He on the other hand, had probably been laughing all along at our gullibility. That rankled! Why couldn't he at least *look* like a villain? (He did, actually, I realized when I saw him later on TV. Without his disguise, his bald head, sagging facial muscles and obnoxious sneer showed no resemblance to the man who had wooed and married Faith LaBounty.)

Betty had slipped out during our discussion with Jameson and had waylaid Mae Willoughby and Don Urquhart before they could leave for home. They were apprehensive as she brought them back to Douglas' office, and after Jameson had left, Douglas told them about Faith's death. He felt that they should be the first to know, to prepare them for the reactions of others when the news was made public. Mae broke down, and after comforting prayer by Douglas, and the promise that he would visit her, Betty drove her home.

Don paced restlessly, chain-smoking. After uttering numerous regrets about having been conned into being Clive Hawthorne's best man, he finally changed the subject.

"I wonder what'll happen about the will Faith made in Clive's favour?"

"I imagine it'll be declared invalid," I replied. "'Clive Hawthorne' wasn't a real person."

"Also, I've heard that you can't benefit from a crime."

"I think that's right."

"But what happens when that will is thrown out? Does her previous one stay in effect?"

"I'm not a lawyer, but I would think it should. If the later will isn't valid, then I'd presume that it would be considered to have never existed. Therefore the old one would still be good."

Don gazed upward as if he could see through the ceiling. "This church could sure use a new roof."

That afternoon, Penny called me, excitement and mirth bubbling in her voice. "Guess what?"

"Now what?" I groaned.

Penny laughed. "It's not what you're thinking."

"Okay. What?"

"Zane and a woman accountant who Zane says you know are forming a partnership to run Owen's business. Actually, the business belongs to a brother, but he isn't an accountant. The woman's name is Virginia Meredith. Do you know her?"

"Yes, I know Ginny. She's my accountant and her husband rents planes from me."

"Is she good?"

"Very."

"That's swell. I guess she will do the accounting and Zane will handle the computer end."

"It ought to work out. I think Zane is probably one of those people with a nose for a good business deal. Ginny's husband, Wilf, is a lawyer, so he ought to make sure everything is done properly. I think it's great. By the way, I met Owen's brother and liked him very much. He's one of those big, honest outdoorsman types who is very direct in his business dealings."

"Great! Anyway, this'll mean that Zane will stay here. And that means that I've got to decide how often I dare to spend a night with him."

"You don't sound very distressed about it, so I'll leave the decision up to you."

I let myself into the darkened church, using a key that Shirley Meacham, the secretary, had given me. Only a few low wattage night lights were on. I found the panel of light switches, and turned on those that lit the chancel and the front-most pews. I also turned on the floodlights on the exterior of the church that illuminated the magnificent stained glass windows at the east and west ends. I lit the candles on the altar, remembering to do the one on the Epistle side before the one on the Gospel side. I stood there and drank in the beauty of the old stone church.

For Compline, we generally congregated around the north side near the front. The person leading the service used one of the prayer desks on the north side of the chancel. Douglas always gave his homily from memory, standing in front of us, outside the communion rail. I knew I couldn't do that, but I didn't want to climb clear up to the pulpit, so I found Elspeth Dodderington's music stand and set it in front of the pews. I placed my sermon, which I had typed on my computer, on the stand. Then I arranged the *Book of Common Prayer*, opened to the proper page, and with the page for the psalm marked, on the prayer desk alongside the book with the scripture readings. I'd find someone to do the readings as people gathered for the service.

I stood back and surveyed the set-up. Had I forgotten anything? Oh, yes. The collect for the day from the leaflet we had gotten in church that morning. I fished a leaflet out of my handbag and found the collect. All was ready.

People began to drift in. The Meachams, Don Urquhart, Penny, tiny little Eleanor Ware, and Elspeth Dodderington. Good! When she was here, we sang the Nunc Dimittis; otherwise we merely read it together. I asked Penny and Eleanor to do the scripture readings.

I heard Douglas' voice, and with his, another voice that made my heart leap with joy. Chris Whitney had come. The Forsythes sat several rows back, behind everyone else, and Chris nervously sat near them, but a few spaces over. I went to her and welcomed her, introducing her to the others.

At 7 o'clock, we began.

"The Lord Almighty grant us a quiet night and a perfect end," I began, and everyone chorused, "Amen." The familiar liturgy rolled easily from our mouths. We said the psalm together, and the readers performed with reverence and skill. Elspeth got up to lead us in the Nunc Dimittis, also known as the Song of Simeon.

Lord, now lettest thou thy servant depart in peace,
according to thy word.
For mine eyes have seen thy salvation, which thou
hast prepared before the face of all people;
To be a light to lighten the gentiles, and to be the
glory of thy people Israel.
Glory be to the Father, and to the Son, and to the
Holy Ghost;
As it was in the beginning, is now, and ever
shall be, world without end. Amen.

The familiar words of the ancient song, words said by Simeon, who had been promised by God that he would not die until he had seen the Messiah, on seeing the baby Jesus, hung in the air and I let them stay there before I continued on.

"Preserve us, O Lord, waking, and guard us sleeping, that awake we may watch with Christ, and asleep we may rest in peace."

It was time for the sermon. I walked around through the central opening in the communion rail, turned and bowed toward the cross on the altar. *Gracious God,* I said to myself, *put your words in my mouth.* Aloud, I said as I crossed myself, "In the name of the Father, and of the Son, and of the Holy Ghost. Amen"

"Amen," came the reply from the pews.

I walked to my makeshift pulpit, stepped back a pace, glanced at the first line I had written, and began, "'He suffered death and was buried. On the third day, he rose again.'"

I paused, then as the familiar words sank in, I went on. "Do you believe this?" I scanned the faces of my audience. They were alert, and distinctly interested.

"You say it in one form or another every Sunday in church. It is part of the Creed. And it is the central theme of our Christian faith. Do you believe what you say?

"If you do, *why* do you believe it? Because the Bible says so? Because you believe that the Bible is the literal word of God, and therefore it must be so?

"Or do you not believe it, because the concept of the physical resurrection of the body after death is foreign to everything you know about death. You have never experienced such a thing — therefore it could not have happened.

"This year, I have been going to church every Sunday, to the Eucharist every Wednesday morning, to morning prayer as often as I could get there and to Bible study, Ash Wednesday and Holy Week services. For the first time, I have heard the story of Jesus' ministry, death and resurrection, and the lives of the apostles — as a whole — in a compact period of time. I have come to realize that, yes, the Bible does say so. Not only does it say in so many words, 'On the third day, he rose again,' but it says so by what we might call circumstantial evidence; by what happened to those who witnessed it."

My little congregation was listening intently. I'd got them hooked all right. Now to reel them in.

"At the beginning of his ministry, Jesus approached ordinary, uneducated peasants and said to them, 'Follow me.' These people left what they were doing, left homes and families, and followed Jesus. For perhaps three years, maybe less, they lived with Jesus, watched Jesus perform miracles, and listened daily to his teaching. It didn't change them very much.

"They misunderstood his teaching, failed to follow his leadership, asked for preferential treatment, quarrelled about who was the greatest. They didn't realize the gravity of the situation when Jesus asked them to pray with him in the Garden of Gethsemane. They fell asleep.

"Jesus patiently explained, chided them for their lack of insight, scolded them for their lack of faith, but never gave up on them.

"Jesus said to Peter, 'Get thee behind me, Satan! You are a stumbling block to me, for you are setting your mind not on divine things, but on human things.' Jesus also said, '...you are Peter, and on this rock I will build my church...'

"Peter — of all people? Peter, who did impulsive things like trying (and failing) to walk on water? Peter — who would deny Jesus three times on the night of Jesus' betrayal, and who would creep off with the others and hide in fear?

"If you had never heard the rest of the story, but were told that these... nitwits ... were to found a church that would reach all the world and endure forever, and that Peter, of all people, would be the leader of that church, might you not say, 'You've got to be kidding!'"

That got a laugh out of them. They were leaning forward intently, hanging on every word.

"After Jesus' death — a very public and unmistakable death — his disciples hid in a locked room, fearing for their lives.

"They were desolate. Their world had collapsed. Their leader was dead and their group began to fall apart.

"And then — something happened. Jesus appeared in their midst.

"At first they didn't recognize him. Just what was different about him is never explained. But they recognized him when he shared a meal with them. Isn't that what we do at every Eucharist? We share a meal with Jesus Christ, and recognize His presence in our midst."

I stopped for a moment and took a deep breath. The words were flowing easily. I had never before felt this good while speaking in public.

"He stayed with his disciples only a short while, and then the Holy Spirit was poured out on them. *Now* they understood. *Now* they believed. *Now* they acted. They went out *boldly* to proclaim the word of the Lord, — to take his teaching to every part of their known world and to *all* people.

"Not just one or two of them. *All* of them. Not for a week, or a month, or a year, but for the rest of their lives. They did this in the face of ridicule and scorn, of apathy and disbelief, of persecution, of torture and even death. None of them backed down. None of them gave up.

"Yes! The Bible tells me that the resurrection really happened. It tells the story of the actions of the followers of Jesus, before and after his death. I cannot think of any other event that could possibly produce such a *profound, absolute* and *enduring* change in them, than to have witnessed the actual physical resurrection of our Lord, Jesus Christ!

"Thomas didn't believe! Not until he had seen and touched the wounds. Then his capitulation was complete.

"'My Lord and my God!'

"Jesus said to him, 'Have you believed because you have seen me?' Millions of people down through the centuries have not had the privilege that Thomas had. To them Jesus has said, 'Blessed are those who have not seen and yet have come to believe.'"

I raised my head and looked Douglas right in the eye.

"I still don't *understand* the Resurrection, but, yes, I believe!"

I stepped back from my makeshift pulpit, walked to the front of the altar, bowed, and resumed my place at the prayer desk. A muted buzz of excited conversation went around the small gathering. I dared not look at them now.

"Please stand as we recite the Creed." Was it my imagination, or was the Creed said with a lot more fervour than usual?

The rest of the service went by like a dream. At the conclusion, my friends gathered round me, shook my hand and expressed delight at my sermon.

"About a third of the way through," Eleanor Ware said, "God came down and spoke through you." I thought back. Yes, she was right. That's when it really began to flow. I had lost all trace of nervousness and could remember with great clarity exactly what I wanted to say. I'd hardly used the notes.

I made my way through the group to where Betty and Douglas stood near the back. Douglas wrapped his arms around me and gave me a discrete kiss on the cheek. "That was wonderful, Robin."

Over his shoulder, I caught sight of Chris Whitney. Her face was a study. On it were registered amazement, awe, excitement, hope and joy; but mixed with those were anxiety and even fear. I knew exactly what she was going through.

I'd been there myself!

About the Author

Anne Barton is a retired veterinarian and flight instructor. In her retirement, she has taken up writing mystery novels. She has also written one autobiographical book and numerous articles and short stories. Her short story won the Bloody Words Crime Writers' Conference contest in 2001 and is published in Bloody Words, The Anthology.

Born in Drumheller, Alberta, she grew up in Northern Idaho, returned to Canada, and now lives in the beautiful Okanagan Valley in British Columbia, where she is deeply involved with Habitat for Humanity and her Anglican Church work – that is, when she isn't riding horses or curling.

217

Made in the USA
Charleston, SC
21 June 2015